D1445973

The Last Estate

The Last Estate

Conor Bowman

THE PERMANENT PRESS
Sag Harbor, NY 11963

For information, address:
  The Permanent Press
  4170 Noyac Road
  Sag Harbor, NY 11963
  www.thepermanentpress.com

Library of Congress Cataloging-in-Publication Data

  Bowman, Conor.
    The last estate / Conor Bowman.
      p. cm.
    ISBN 978-1-57962-203-9 (hardcover : alk. paper)
      1. Teenage boys—Fiction. 2. Married women—Fiction.
    3. Provence (France)—Fiction. I. Title.

  PR6052.O889L37 2010
  823'.914—dc22   2010012542

Printed in the United States of America.

For Charlie Bowman,
my whist partner and wrestling opponent

ACKNOWLEDGEMENTS

I would like to express my gratitude and appreciation to a number of people who helped me in some way in the writing of this book:

Mary Honan, Mary P. Guinness, Celine Sheridan, John Murphy, Sylvie Archimbaud, Robert & Francoise Leterrier, Roger Sweetman, Dearbhla Ní Ghríofa, George Allen (sadly now deceased), Catherine Higgins, Annette Foley, Mark de Blacam, Siobhan Gallagher, Fabienne Pleyben, Colette Griffin, Colette Crus et sa famille à Gigondas, Pat & Ann O'Malley, Annie Leonard, Auntie Betty, Liz James, Monique Rigney, Florence Kponsou, Elizabeth McSharry and Anthony Previté.

Joy Kleinstuber travelled to Gigondas to undertake invaluable and in-depth research. Mary Kelly was a huge help; she provided firsthand information about the art of winemaking and makes great wine herself at Domaine du Pech Rome.

The village of Gigondas in the southern Rhône Valley is the inspiration for this novel. As a teenager I spent part of the summer of 1979 there on an exchange. It held a magical quality for me then and continues to do so.

Finally, I would like to express my deepest gratitude to Marty and Judith Shepard, Rania Haditirto, Joslyn Pine, Susan Ahlquist, and everyone else at The Permanent Press, for showing faith in me and my writing.

CHAPTER ONE

When I was nine years old, a boy at school cut me on the left side of my face with a hunting knife, in a fight about nothing.

"You don't even own a dog," he said.

"Yes, I do," I replied, "Mangetout."

"He's not yours. He belongs to your brother."

"We *both* own him."

The air between us grew damp with argument and we crossed the divide and fought as if we were two mongrels. A crowd of our school comrades encircled us, each boy calling out the name of the warrior he supported. In the heart of the fight, my opponent pulled out a knife and I was injured. I think the wounding frightened him even more than it did me; the battle ended the instant blood had been drawn.

The scar was three-and-a-half centimetres long and it lay diagonally across the top of my cheek, pointing simultaneously at my left eye and the bottom of my left earlobe. *Cicatrice* is the French word for a scar and for a while people called me that as a nickname. I didn't mind the nickname, it's not the worst. I suppose I don't even really mind the scar itself.

By the time I was almost seventeen, and in my last year in the village lycée, the scar had grown slightly longer, but also more vague, as my skin tightened and stretched the cicatricial line to its thinnest. The boy who slashed me died from tuberculosis in 1914. He was eleven. His name was Yves Couderc. Less than a month after they'd buried him, the war began.

The last time I'd seen him he was shopping in the village square with his mother. He'd been waiting for her outside the bakery, and he stood beside a small grey poodle that was

9

tied by its leash to the handle of one of the double doors. Yves was coughing into a handkerchief. Over his hand, in the bunch of cotton that resembled an opened flower, small flecks of red mottled the hem. It was the only time in two years that he hadn't pretended to smile secretly to himself about my scar when we'd met. It was the only time, in those two years too, that I hadn't tried to hide my left cheek from his view. There was something special about that shared moment in the village square which has remained with me to this day. Some strange, almost barely perceptible thought or emotion passed between us and it was as if we knew we were saying goodbye. He nodded a greeting and I acknowledged it in return. I then discreetly allowed my attention to be drawn elsewhere, in order to permit him to continue his bloody coughing in peace. Even the small dog looked away. Nobody wants to catch a glimpse of death if they can avoid it.

To BE legally classed as *Côtes de Rhône-Villages*, wine from this region has to be made from at least twenty-five percent of Syrah, Mourvèdre and Cinsault grapes. It is less clear what the blood of a person must contain to be classed as local. What I do know is that my great-grandfather served under Napoleon at Waterloo and that made us locals of all France. Our family prided itself on its heritage, and I suppose, that was a start. Nothing comforts us in the present perhaps, so much as the knowledge that our forebears endured hardship and survived. We draw solace from the gene pool. It grants us continuity. We live side-by-side in the here and now, confident that the march of progress and industry has fashioned a slightly more cushioned world. That is the theory at least.

In 218 B.C., Hannibal passed through Provence and then on to the Alps. In 1720, The Great Plague crept north from Marseille and devastated the region. In 1918, on a Sunday in October, the Germans proposed an armistice and yet the war did not end for some weeks after that. This region, with its holm oaks and olives and cypress and almond trees, has always been holding its breath, just as the entire nation did that October. Good news usually seems too good to be true here. When the waiting is over, the confirmation of that news is usually overtaken by some greater and darker realisation: that things are actually worse because of the news we waited for but never got to enjoy.

Forest fires, when they occur, drive with the wind and the drought and often only stop at the coast. There are few mountains, but here in the department known as Vaucluse, the Dentelles provide a backdrop for the minute portion of this country which I really call home. You can smell the lavender all summer. In the winter, the small cloth bags of it usher the scent out the doors of every wardrobe. This is the place where I spent all of my time and my energies as a boy, trying to understand the entirety of the outside world through my small experiences in the village of Gigondas.

Our home is a château on the western approach road to the village. It was called Montmirail, after the tallest peak in the mountain range that hugs the village to the east like a surprise embrace in a shop. It is not really a castle, but it is the largest house in the village. It earned its title of château more by default than anything else. It is a grand building with a tree-lined avenue that sweeps rather impressively up from the main road to Sablet, a neighbouring village. The house was reputedly built in medieval times on the site of the wedding-ring exchange of Pierre of Provence and Princess Maguelone of Naples. Legend has it that the couple travelled to the Dentelles from Aigues-Mortes where Pierre had been restored to health by the princess. She had turned her hand to charitable works as a way to forget her previous unhappy love. True or not, we all believed it and it made Montmirail even more special than it already was.

The house has six bedrooms, and an enormous dining room on the ground floor with south-facing windows which suck in the sunshine all year round. It is built of local stone, and the outside walls are imbued with a sort of russet solidity that is typical of Provence. The roll-tiles on the roof are the colour of sunset and the house is clearly visible from the summit of its namesake in the Dentelles. From the air I imagine it resembles a red tortoise, sleeping at the entrance to the village.

Our village is like thousands of others. It has a café, a small hotel, a school, a bakery and a town hall. There, the mayor, Monsieur Gustave de Vay, kept a tiny office which allowed him refuge from a wife he'd never loved. Each year, in the mellow September heat, on the feast of St. Cosme and St. Damien, all the inhabitants of the village gathered to hear the priest deliver his sermon, dressed in his ceremonial robes. Later on, in the evening, after the magnificent feast at the fountain, we would all stand and stare up into the benign Provençal sky and wait, while a member of the police from the station at Carpentras supervised the fireworks display. It was perfect, and in September 1919 it was no less so, in the first celebration of this feast day since the war.

"Christian," Miss Pleyben the geography teacher said, as she touched me on the shoulder at the display. "Some day that will be you. You'll be the one setting off the fireworks."

I turned around, and saw her lovely face illuminate, and then become dark, as the Catherine wheels and fizz rockets exploded and died away above us. She was slightly shorter than I was, with long hair the colour of sunlight. Her shapely body was gathered in at the waist, as a curtain might be by a drape holder, and her eyes sparkled all the time as if she knew something she wasn't yet prepared to share. Sometimes her face was sad, as if she were remembering when really she'd rather not. But the combination of all of the elements comprising her was a person whom it would be impossible not to notice in a crowd.

Everybody knew that her husband had left her because he was about to be conscripted. He was an evil man who beat her so regularly that it was almost shocking to finally see her natural beauty when she no longer needed makeup to hide the bruises. On one occasion, years earlier, I'd seen them arguing in the square and he'd raised his hand to strike her. He'd noticed me standing there and had allowed his hand to make some mawkish false diversion to his own head, where he smoothed down his generous allocation of greasy hair.

Most of the other teachers occasionally called me *Cicatrice*, or mentioned my scar in some oblique nasty way, but not Miss Pleyben. I wanted to hurry up and grow into a man so that I could marry her. I would take care of her and love her and never ever treat her badly, and she'd never have to spend another sou on mascara. I would lie with her, and well, you know— And in the mornings I'd bring her breakfast in bed and make her coffee with fresh milk and black coffee beans from the market in Sablet.

"Yes, Miss," I answered. "Someday that will be me."

The lifeblood of the region is wine, and my family have been winemakers for more than two centuries. In 1672, when the original—and smaller—house was built on the same site, it was a very similar terrain which bordered the foothills of the Dentelles. The soil is not much good for anything except vines and olives. As a result, the area has developed in the only direction open to it. The massive granite, pudding-shaped stones, which give an impression of being unwelcome where cultivation is concerned, in reality play an important part in the successful production of wine in the area. These stones, in areas where the vine has been established, act as reflectors and direct the sun back onto the grapes. The end result is big, high-in-alcohol reds, and even some respectable rosés. The eleven-and-a-half hectares attached to Montmirail produce deep red wine every year. The cellars are among the oldest in France and even predate the original house.

I have to say, though, that this weight of tradition was not sufficient to convince me of my role in its continuation. That belief is perhaps at the heart of my story and my life. I never believed that just because something is one particular way that it must remain so forever. I cry out for the right of the individual, the self, the soul, to reach out past itself and into the hearts of others, rather than to constantly look back over its own shoulder. I yearn for the freedom of spirit, the latitude, the opportunity in myself and in everyone else, to become what we want, and to refuse to continue to be who and what we are if those manifestations do not reflect our own desires. I believe most of all in the inherent capacity man and woman possess to change.

In the countryside, where the village is the kingdom and the child is the peasant, the father is king. The son is like a granite rock on the edge of a vineyard; his job is to reflect, and his destiny is to remain in that place forever. The only power higher than man is God, so that even in the kingdom the high priest is sometimes the real king for a time.

Despite the separation of church and state common to most areas in France by that time, the power of the land-owning class was still very much in evidence. The Jesuits owned the school, and their trade-off for nominal rent was to insist on at least a modicum of religious instruction by one of their number to every class. As I progressed through the lycée, the classes became smaller and smaller; people drifted out of the education system and back into their farms, having mastered the ability to count, and read road signs and medication labels.

Father Leterrier was a Jesuit. He came twice a month from the monastery at Crillon-le-Brave on the other side of the Dentelles, to give us religious instruction. He was a tall, almost elegant-looking priest with an air of great confidence and self-importance. He also possessed a religious fervour that he was unable to impart to his students. As I grew tired in my early teens of attending his classes at all, Fr. Leterrier seemed to grow commensurately more and more interested in his students' moral welfare so that, in my last two years at the lycée, the lessons he taught us dealt solely with the moral state of near-perfection that he called "Holy Purity":

"Puberty marks a dangerous time; its onset heralds untold hazards. The young adult is faced with desires and impulses infinitely more evil than those which tempted our forefathers in more guarded and disciplined times. Holy Purity is known as the Angelic Virtue because it is the quality which most makes man like the angels. It is the most precious of possessions. Purity—the very word is redolent of sacrifice and self-control."

This man, who had begun our religious instruction years earlier with lively stories about Noah and the Ark and the struggles of Daniel and David, began to transform before our eyes, on a twice-monthly basis, into an obsessive fanatic. His every waking moment seemed dedicated to the care of a warped ideal he had planted years earlier in some earthenware pot deep in his churning heart. For the girls, he was twice-monthly menstrual pain.

"Have no doubt about it; temptation will attempt to enter your hearts. The enemies of Christ make battering rams from the debris of hope. They fashion siege machinery from the arrogance which promiscuity begets. The offspring of the Damned are the foot-soldiers of this onslaught. You must fight against these powers and temptations with every last ounce and drop of your strength and blood. Leave no avenue unexplored in your quest for sustenance against the herd of evil Satan sends to do his work. The pure of heart will be the bulwark in Christ's battleships. But those who falter, and succumb to the pleasures of the flesh, are no longer fit company for Heaven. A failure to obey Christ's teachings in any way whatsoever, but in particular in matters of Holy Purity, renders the soul of the individual transgressor abhorrent to God. To die in such a state would be a disaster beyond description!"

I wondered if Yves Couderc had died in such a state. Had his actions, in scarring me, marked his own soul out as unfit for Heaven? I was terrified that because we'd never made up the argument, never spoken of forgiveness, I might have unwittingly condemned him to eternity in a furnace. Perhaps I should have gone to him and said, "It's alright, I don't mind the scar, it's not the worst." Would this have wiped his slate clean? Did God send him sickness because of his sin? I just didn't know; yet I harboured a residual hope in a corner of my mind that somehow, the last time I'd seen him, the glance that passed between us might have meant more than goodbye.

When I was fifteen-and-a-half, I went one July evening to the Chapel of Saint Cosme, on the small hill on the Vacqueyras Road. I pushed open the warm wooden door and made my way inside. As usual, the place was empty. It was just myself and God, and the chipped statue of Saint Cosme with its flickering wax candles on the brass stand in front of the side-altar. I knelt in the front row on an embroidered kneeler which was old and red. In a way, I suppose, I thought that the further up the church I went, the closer to Him I'd be. I told Him that I didn't mind the scar at all and that I wished Couderc well, wherever he was.

"You know, God, if you cast your mind back to that day I saw him for the last time, outside the bakery, I'm sure you probably thought that I was only saying goodbye to him, or something like that, when we looked at each other and nodded. It may have looked that way, but what I was actually thinking, in my mind, and my heart, was that I forgave him. I didn't realise it at the time, but later on, looking back, I'm pretty sure too that he was saying I'm sorry to me. I know he *was* sorry, although he never actually *said* the words. Anyway, I just thought I'd let you know in case you watched that day and weren't sure that the whole scar thing had been settled for good before he died. I know you're pretty busy, what with looking after all the people who have died in the war and everything. My mother used to say before the war that when the winter comes, you get really busy. But you probably haven't had a moment to draw your breath for a long time. I have to go now, but just one last thing: if you get a chance, say hello to Mangetout for me and tell Eugene that I hope he doesn't mind that I got his room."

I heard a noise behind me, as though there was someone watching, but when I looked around there was no one there. I had to get home for supper so I left, but the door was ajar and I'd been fairly sure I had closed it when I'd entered the chapel. Maybe God was saying "I hear you." Maybe He actually does listen sometimes.

MY LIFE, for the most part, up until the time Couderc died, had been happy. I suppose that the people who complain by saying, 'Oh I can't complain,' or, 'I'm looking on the best side,' are really only happy when they *are* complaining; but I have to say that my own life was happy. I draw a line across my life at Couderc's death, but if I am truthful, or if a mental doctor of psycho-whatever-they-are were to examine my head and grope around my thoughts for a bit, then my childhood probably ended a little bit later.

On the twenty-fifth of February 1916, my brother Eugene was killed in action near Verdun, at the battle which led to the fall of Fort Douaumont. It was then that my life, as I now have it, really began. I looked up in geography class that day, at a quarter-past-two in the cold afternoon, thinking I'd heard a scream. I saw that everyone else was still writing silently and attentively, having apparently heard nothing. Miss Pleyben glanced around for a moment from the blackboard and smiled when she saw me. I smiled too. It was our moment, like that time with Couderc, only better. I've always wondered since whether I heard my brother scream as he died. If it was his voice I heard, then Miss Pleyben was with me when Eugene died, and this has only served to reinforce my affection for her.

My mother was an enigmatic woman in many ways because she never told us what she really thought. It was her post in our house to tread the thin line between her loyalty to my father and her affection for Eugene. She stayed at that post until it was no longer necessary to make the choice she'd always really stopped short of making anyway. She was a beautiful woman, untouchable in that eternal way which actresses often have about them. She had the face of an angel, and yet her eyes were always sad.

She was not from Provence; she was a Breton, from Plougerneau, in the northwest of Brittany. She always said that she missed the rain. I remember how once, when I was God-knows-how-small and in her arms—or perhaps in a cradle with her leaning over me—that she cried the most perfect tear and it absconded down her cheek. It lingered before it dropped down onto my face and I tasted salt for the first time. Even now, I recall that experience and I think again, as always, that I have tasted the sea on the rain from the place where my mother was born.

Those delightful people, with their own language and their ties to Celtic mysticism and the sea, lay then and lie now in the background like a chorus line at the end of the performance: too happy for words, too unhappy for silence. My mother held the line, and when she no longer had to do that, she retreated to her room at the back of Montmirail, to wait for death and the intermissions of cold love my father rationed, even after the war had ended.

On Christmas morning, 1916, I came downstairs at the same moment when my parents were in the dining room exchanging presents; I stood quietly by, a silent onlooker. Maman had made him a jacket from light grey material she had scavenged from somewhere. He wore it as if he were a peacock, twisting this way and that to see himself in the mirror. My mother stood by, meekly, admiring him and sharing in his happiness.

"Your gift is in the box on the table," he told her.

Maman unwrapped the ribbon from around the package. Inside, a long red dress lay folded in on itself. As she held it to her shoulders it was clear, even to me, that it was far too small to fit her. She stood there, bathed in uncertainty, not wishing to seem ungrateful, and perhaps frightened that he might ask her to try it on. She need not have concerned herself in that regard.

"You know there's a war on, Helene. Try to eat a little less. For France."

My mother began to sob quietly.

"You cruel bastard," I shouted from the doorway. He spun round, clearly embarrassed at having been observed in this act of malice. He said nothing, but simply walked out of the room past me.

That afternoon, just as we sat down to dinner, he looked across the table at me and spoke as he carved.

"Christian, the dog caught its paw in a trap. It was in too much pain." I discovered later that he'd taken Mangetout's head off, with an axe, as an act of 'mercy.'

For my father, the only warmth lay in wine. Not in his consumption of it, but its consuming him. He lived solely for himself. Anyone who would reflect glory back at him was welcome, in the cruellest of ways, to catch the light and turn it back upon him day or night, until they dimmed from the effort and he glowed from their sacrifice. For Robert Aragon, the world narrowed into a point that almost touched his feet. He was the king of a dynasty that stretched out behind him like a cape in the wind. Almost all of his expectations had been fulfilled. His two final quests were to prepare his heir for the throne, by any means necessary, and to die clutching that most elusive of all viticultural plaudits—the *Medaille d'Or* from the *Concours National*, which was held in Paris each July.

He was a man capable of enforcing his worldview with violence, and I was often the 'beneficiary' of his method of education. On the day of Couderc's funeral, my father came into my room in the afternoon. I was sitting on the edge of the bed and it was clear that I had been crying.

"I suppose you've been whingeing about that boy they buried. The one who gave you the scar." I looked up, but said nothing. "You know he probably already had the disease when you fought with him, so you shouldn't blame yourself. Anyway, he's gone now and you're still alive."

I dried my eyes and began to stand up, but a punch in the face from him laid me flat on my back.

"You selfish little pup. You didn't even have the courtesy to go to his funeral. What do you think people will say about our family *now*?"

"But, Papa, I—" I tried to explain myself to him, but it was no use. He never listened to any voice other than his own. Next day at school, people asked me about my black eye. I told them I'd walked into a door.

Everybody has some kind of scar, and I have already explained how I came to have mine. Lines drawn across my face divide my horizons—mark the end of my childhood and the beginning of another phase—these fractions of my life all blur together if I am honest now. In fact, the only line that meant anything to me was the one drawn across my life by fate, on the day I finally realised that I was in love with my geography teacher, Vivienne Pleyben.

CHAPTER TWO

"I'm not a big fan of Algerians." My father spoke as he lifted a forkful of pork to his fat mouth at dinnertime in early May, 1920. He'd put on weight since the war had ended.

"Why not?" I asked innocently, knowing the answer before I'd even formed the question.

"They're not French," he stated bluntly and patronisingly, as though there could be no other rational answer.

"Neither are the Americans and they helped us win the war."

"Don't be facetious, you know what I mean," he snapped.

"Oh," I said, with an accusing expression.

"Your father doesn't like to talk about the war," my mother said gently. "Robert, would you like some more meat?"

My father held out his plate, like a child might, and my mother scurried off to the kitchen to replenish it. While she was gone we sat in silence, averting our eyes from each other and our hands from any condiment on the table where they might meet. We truly had nothing in common beyond our name.

Eugene had been my father's firstborn, and consequently, all Robert Aragon's dreams and hopes had been centered upon him. He had only been eighteen when he was killed and would remain eighteen forever. I, on the other hand, was nearly seventeen then and had a lifetime of disappointing my father ahead of me. We both knew it. When my mother said that he did not like to talk about the war, what she really meant was that he did not like others to talk about the war.

He mentioned it himself at every opportunity, but that was permissible because in my father's mind only three Frenchmen had actually taken full part in the war: Eugene,

Marshal Pétain and, of course, my father himself. It was risible really, but he almost certainly believed it, although, of course, he was never foolish enough to express it in those terms. From his conversation and demeanour, it was clear that somewhere along the way they all must have met up, perhaps in a café, and drawn lots to decide their plan of action. As it happened, Pétain was chosen to survive the war, Eugene to be killed in it and Robert Aragon to stay at home and contemplate, alternately, the enormity of both death and survival. The suffering of war was justified by a young corporal in 1915 who wrote home, *I suffer, yes I suffer, but so be it. I offer up my life in expiation of my sins and those of France.* The Church and my father joined hands in inducting Eugene into immortality. The countless others whose names they did not know would have to rely on their families for their own dose of salvation.

"Algerians are the scum of the earth," my father said, when my mother returned with a second helping. We all knew that the learned commentary on Algerians had been prompted by the arrival in the village of a family from Algiers. The father was going to work on one of the other local vineyards, Domaine de la Mavette. It seemed incredible to me then, in 1920, a mere two years after the war had ended, that the differences between races would still excite hatred in this small-minded way. What exactly had Eugene been fighting for? So that we could defeat the Germans and be free once again to hate in our own language people who were different? People of other races were rare in Gigondas. But why should they not be instantly liked because of their difference, rather than reviled? It hinted at something in my father's makeup that was awry, but I was too young to be able to catch and describe it that summer.

"When does school finish, Christian?" My mother brokered a peace at the table with a smile and an innocuous question.

"July the twenty-sixth," I answered.

"You'll be able to begin working then," my father stated.

It was not a question. It was, in his mind at any rate, a fact. Eugene was gone and I would have to do as an heir to the business. I didn't answer him directly.

"May I be excused, Maman? I have other things to do."

"Of course, Chéri." My mother smiled in her shy frightened way. We all knew that the subject would come up for discussion again sooner or later.

I walked outside near the seized-up grape-press in the courtyard at the heart of Montmirail. George Phavorin, my father's foreman, was loading barrels of wine onto a cart for the weekly trip to the railway station at Sablet. From there the wine would go to Orange and onwards to Paris or Marseille.

"You're not at school today?" he asked with a smile.

"Half-day Wednesday. Remember?"

He was an enormous man with hands like baker's shovels. For most of my life, he'd lived in the workman's cottage on the road to the sulphur springs at Les Florets and came to work at Montmirail every single day. My father never gave him credit for his real worth; but there was nothing novel in that. Without George Phavorin, Montmirail would have come to a standstill. If he knew it himself he never said anything, and so it was impossible to discern even if he did know whether he was resentful.

"Want to come to Sablet?" he asked, heaving the last barrel on top of two more at the back of the cart where they made a pyramid. I thought of my school project in geography on which I had yet to make a start. It was warm and I was in no mood for burying my head in books for the rest of the afternoon. As an answer to his question, I climbed into the driver's seat and began to untie the long reins.

"Move over, Cowboy," he said with a laugh, as he swung effortlessly onto the seat beside me. He clicked his tongue, and the two horses stopped sleeping and began to amble toward the archway at the back of the property. As we edged out onto the track behind the large barn, the house came sharply into view and we could see my mother at an upstairs window, pretending to close the shutters.

"How are things with you and your father?" George asked.

"The same," I replied. "Always the same."

Behind us, the giant teeth of the mountain range soaked up the heat and I turned my head to see whether I could catch a glimpse of Miss Pleyben's house, way above the church and the cemetery. It was like a buffer, halfway from the village to the foothills, a border of sorts between man and nature. I loved her with all my heart and she didn't know a thing about it. My project would have to be the best ever. I might even win the prize of an outing to Avignon if I worked hard enough. I'd make her proud. So proud. I knew she'd never love me back, but in a way that was half of the challenge.

It pained me to think of my future, because the little of it I could see looked fairly bleak. The innuendo of the table talk that lunchtime was only a sniff of the battle yet to come. I did not know whether I would even be strong enough to take part in that struggle. Winning it certainly was not an option. If only Eugene hadn't been killed. Things would have been so much better. I remembered sitting with him, years earlier, on the wall near the fever hospice, during the school holidays.

"You're the one he loves," I said. "He can't stand me."

"It's because you remind him of himself."

I never understood Eugene's response.

"Want to know a secret?" George said, with a grin, as we passed the *grangeons* on the Sablet road. Tired ploughs and carts hid in these half-houses waiting to be useful again.

"Sure," I replied.

"You're going to be someone great when you grow up."

"What's the secret, George?"

"That is the secret," he said, laughing.

"I think you're very greatly mistaken."

"No, no I mean it. You'll be another Napoleon, a Pétain, or maybe a great writer, like Victor Hugo."

"You got me all figured out wrong, George." I smiled. "I'm not going to be anybody at all when I grow up."

"You mark my words." He wagged his finger in my face.

I felt the scar on my cheek and thought of Couderc. He'd not really had the chance to grow up. Would he have been someone great if his lungs had been luckier? Who knows?

Ahead of us on the road we saw the *diligence*, owned by Monsieur Vaton, carrying its passengers to Sablet to catch the train to Orange. From the back it looked like a large funeral carriage, and again I thought about Eugene and remembered *his* funeral. Without a body, the ceremony had seemed to me to be a farce, with his summer uniform and a handful of letters in a warm box made of cedar wood. A half-hour crammed with prayers and tears. I tried to imagine now, as I had then, his real self, the body which had contained his laugh and his voice buried in a mass grave near Fort Douaumont. It would be lifeless, of course, but warm perhaps, surrounded by comrades who had died quickly or slowly—depending. How had Eugene died? For me, as for the younger brothers of every other soldier who had been killed, I suppose the only solace was in the thought that he might have died instantly and without pain. I envisioned some carpenter's son from a village in Bavaria lining up my brother in his sights and then, 'snap,' as death and sleep arrived on a bullet. It was too horrible to imagine any other scenario. Sometimes, I even believed that he was still alive and that he would come walking up the avenue at Montmirail on leave, with his gun over his shoulder and some unusual confectionery in his pockets from a shop in the north.

The last time he'd been home had been in October, 1915. He'd arrived out of the blue and only stayed four days before being summoned back to the front.

"Tell me about the Germans," I'd asked, excitedly. He was sitting on the bed in my room overlooking the courtyard.

"I don't know much about them, really. They have enormous cannon that fire shells bigger than wine casks."

If only everyone had been drenched in red wine instead of blood.

"What are you daydreaming about?" George thumped me playfully on the back, and I returned to May, 1920.

"Nothing, George. Nothing."

"I don't believe you," he said. "You've got so much going on in that head of yours. Probably planning for your exams, eh?"

"Maybe."

George smiled and encouraged the horses to increase their pace as we caught sight of the mill on the edge of Sablet. In the distance, way off and over to our left, lay the simple solid railway bridge over the Ouveze marking the midpoint between Sablet and Violes. Rivers and railways were an integral part of geography, but nowhere near as important as the woman who taught the subject to us. I was sure that I had been in her class at the very instant Eugene had been killed. That surely was more omen than coincidence? Father Leterrier, with all his claptrap about morality and his talk of 'desires and impulses infinitely more evil,' knew absolutely nothing about love. How could he, hidden away in that monastery at Crillon-le-Brave, emerging twice a month to preach morals to unsuspecting adolescents? What did he know about anything, besides loneliness and the myth of miracles? How did he even know if there was a God?

Outside the railway station was a small square, and each Wednesday the market there drew large numbers. When we arrived it was nearly over. The stalls were mostly empty. One of the vendors, still going strong, was shouting.

"Chanoux coffee; one-franc-fifty a quarter."

He was a small man with a moustache that bisected his face and headed for his ears. Behind him the butcher was closing up shop, and only a couple of dead pigeons hung from the stand over the bloodstained marble counter. Pretty much everyone else was finished, and the cauliflower leaves, rotting at their edges in the gutter, had long since said goodbye to their heads. At the entrance to the railway station, the front page from the previous week's edition of *Le Ventoux* announced: HERNIA CURED BY THE LEROY METHOD. HÔTEL DU COMMERCE, VAISON, ON THE EIGHTH OF JUNE NEXT. ALL WELCOME.

George and I unloaded the barrels and rolled them through the narrow archway past the ticket office and onto the platform. While George spoke to the loading officer and obtained a receipt, the train lay panting on the tracks, with steam escaping in bursts from the dull-green engine funnel. Two of the five carriages were about half-filled with passengers, and the other three were at near-capacity with goods. Four men in light blue overalls were working full-tilt, loading and unloading. Sacks of flour and bales of wool were taken from the train and laid side by side on the platform, while barrels of wine and bales of silk were made ready to take their place. As the train pulled out of the station, George and I stood together and watched it chug slowly past the signal box and on towards Orange. The sun seemed warmer now than it had at midday.

"It's tough work," said George. "How about a beer?"

"Okay."

I wanted to do anything that would delay the trip back home. The remaining stalls in the market were now closed. We left the horses tied outside the station. We walked into the village to a bar where there was only one customer apart from ourselves, a tiny grey-haired man with a goatee. He'd obviously come from the market, as his overalls were stained with grease. Beside him, knife handles protruded from a wrapping of cloth. Outside, I'd noticed his grindstone mounted on a wooden barrow. He nodded in greeting.

"Two beers." George ordered them from the pretty barmaid behind the counter.

The knife-grinder saw me looking at the bundle beside him. "Want a look?"

"Not really," I said, but my face said, 'Yes, please.'

He lifted the packet and rolled it on the counter. A grim collection of knives and skewers rattled open.

"Don't scratch my bar," said the barmaid. George and I looked at the knives.

"Try one if you like," said the man.

I instinctively ran a finger along my scar, and then picked up a large pocket-knife which was open. I coaxed my thumb over and back on the blade and felt it tease my skin with the double allures of danger and protection.

The knife-man grinned, "Nice, isn't it?"

"Not bad," I said.

"How much?" asked George.

"Fifty francs."

"I'll give you thirty-five." George took the money out of his breast pocket.

The man wanted to say no, to bargain hard, but something, perhaps a bad day at the market, changed his mind.

"You're robbing me, you know. But, all right, thirty-five."

"It's a gift for this young man for helping me bring the barrels to the station."

George paid the agreed price, and I became the owner of a pocket-knife which would make me the envy of all the boys at school.

"He probably got it to sharpen from someone who forgot to collect it," George remarked on the way home, as I held the knife open and tried to make it glint in the sunlight. I thought about bayonets and wondered, if I had a rifle, could I fix the knife to the end of it with wire or something.

Outside Sablet, on the roadside, was a billboard, which advertised a cleaning tool. LIQUID VENEER MOP. WORLD CHAMPION.

"More rubbish," George said, as we passed it.

As we neared Gigondas, I fully appreciated, perhaps for the first time, its uniqueness: rising up into the hills and cocooning around the church at the top of the village. The

Dentelles were grey-white like the stones they sell you for the bath. The towers at the back of Montmirail guided us in a direct line with the village square, Place Gabriel Andeol. The late afternoon sun bathed the whole place in a yellow half-light, where sprinkles of dust floated to us on the wonderful scent of cypress. The soil was the colour of the inside of mushrooms, and somewhere up in the village schoolchildren laughed towards the end of the half-day holiday.

"What next?" George asked, as I jumped down from the cart in the courtyard.

"My geography project," I said, solemnly. "I'm a bit late with it already."

"And she, the teacher, how is she? Good?" he asked.

"The best," I said.

"She'll kill you if you don't get it finished!" He laughed.

"I wouldn't mind. Dying like that wouldn't be too bad."

Chapter Three

"We must beware of certain books. I refer, of course, to books or pamphlets of impure suggestion." Fr. Leterrier droned on and on, but we only really paid attention when he seemed about to deliver some valuable advice. "And where would young people find such books?"

We held our breath. I saw Elise Morel blush, but also hold her pen at the ready to transcribe the directions when given. Joseph Hillion was nudging Abel Beaumet and they giggled like old geese. We waited for the answer. Fr. Leterrier enlightened us.

"They are everywhere to be found that the Devil frequents."

"In the Convent of Prebayon, Father?"

Everyone laughed. Fr. Leterrier became angry and glanced up suddenly from his notes.

"Who said that?"

Charles Ferrier raised his hand and there was silence. The priest looked as if he were going to explode, and began to advance down the room to where Ferrier sat.

"That's just an old woman's story, a myth. It's not true, do you hear me? It's not true." He stared madly at Charles, but the pupil stood his ground and stared back. Just as he reached the boy's desk, the priest seemed to realise that he was too old and the boy too big to be able to impose any physical control over the situation. At the crucial moment, the priest simply leaned over the desk of the student and hissed as he said, "It's not true, I'm telling you, it's not true." Some well-behaved child, in the class below us, rang the handbell in the corridor and the confrontation ended.

It was the first time that we'd seen the priest blow up like that. The Convent, and the story of the Devil building a bridge overnight for the nuns in return for their pledge of allegiance to him, was a local legend. But it was very interesting to witness the priest's reaction to it. Something in the hint of it had clearly unsettled him or shaken his beliefs. It might be useful to us to remember the moment for future reference. At any rate, I was bitterly disappointed not to get more information about where to find books or pamphlets full of impure suggestions. Perhaps they were to be found in my dreams.

I have nearly always been able to fly in my dreams. Since I can remember, the deepest sleep has brought with it travel unimagined and impossible in daylight. I find myself running along the corridor outside my parents' room, and then taking off like an aeroplane out of the front upstairs window over the entrance hall to Montmirail. During the war I'd seen an aeroplane once, at the airfield at Devil's Plain near Gigondas. I don't know if I dreamed I was an aeroplane before I saw one, but when I dream, I soar. I fly out of the domain and over the village, the school and the square. I swoop low to the hotel to watch the birds picking for food behind it, in the courtyard where the scraps are thrown from the kitchen. The birds scatter as I shout. They abandon their meal and lift in all directions, surrounding me for a moment in the air like thieves around a gold watch. I fly for hours over places I've only seen from the roadside. Below me, at the spa of Les Florets, all kinds of deformed and sick people bathe their problems away. Sometimes the waters are empty, and I fly low and feel the heat on my face and smell the sulphur. One time, I flew over George as he was bringing barrels to Sablet in the cart. I'm almost sure he looked up and waved.

For years, school had always left me tired in the evenings; but that summer I found myself full of energy in the afternoons and wishing sometimes that the school day wouldn't end. Even Fr. Leterrier's visits began to interest me on some level. I wasn't sure at first, because until Easter that year I had resented his lectures and had been bored by him. As the summer approached, I felt my attitude changing slowly. At first I felt sympathy for him—an old man among a crowd of people who did not want him or his advice. Gradually, this gave way to my finding the classes humorous. I began to relish the thought that here, in front of us, a celibate wreck was salivating while warning us about the acts he himself probably wanted to engage in but could not. It was a pathetic scene, like the fat man who loves cakes being destined to meet scores of bakers and cream-makers, but forbidden to indulge his addiction. Yes, that was it. I'm sure Fr. Leterrier got some perverse pleasure from talking to us in high tones about morality and purity, but even that precluded him from touching the words he clearly wanted.

I do not know the precise moment when the transformation occurred, but, midway through my last term at the lycée, the same thoughts I had seemed to dawn on others in the class. The girls were the first to have this revelation. Mathilde Bremond began to wear shorter skirts, Julie Saurel's blouse was unbuttoned more than it should have been. Even Elise Morel, whom I had always thought to be saint material, began to walk into religion class in a way that could only send a boy's mind in one direction. The boys too played their part, and like actors who have been in the same ensemble cast for years, drifted effortlessly in and out of the drama which was unfolding.

"Father Leterrier, what will happen to people who stray from the path of Holy Purity?" Abel Beaumet asked one afternoon.

"They will rot in the fires of Hell. Their flesh will melt and all of the impurities in their blood will be filtered onto the floor like a carpet of evil dust." The priest's eyes were wide with rage and envy.

"Why are priests not allowed to marry?" Leopold Palon ventured, one hot Thursday in early June.

The priest's face lodged in regret and he shook his head before answering. "The Church teaches that Jesus was a man and that his disciples were men. As priests, we must keep ourselves pure in every way, so that we can do God's work without the distractions and the sins of the flesh."

"My father says that the total eclipse of the moon, on May second, was God's way of telling us we're not doing enough to please Him," said one of the girls.

"We can never, ever do enough to please Him. We must continually strive to be better people." The priest sounded tired.

The classroom that day was like a cauldron. Even with one of the windows open, the heat shimmered into the room and bathed the group in perspiration. The girls' blouses were damp in patches, and here and there the light revealed the outline of a breast or the shadow of a nipple. The humidity made all the chalk damp and useless. Through the opened window the outside world glistened with sunshine which seemed almost edible. The priest faced us on his chair, but we had become the captors now; we, who were about to storm into adulthood and the huge world beyond this little school, made a statement with our bodies and our minds. We were at the point in our journey when our bodies would cross the divide between guilt and pleasure.

Miss Pleyben's class had always been my favourite. I suppose it must have become my favourite at one particular point in time, after I'd experienced all of the other subjects and their teachers, and made a choice of some sort. You probably have to taste all of the available fruits before settling on the one you like most. Yes, of course, that was logical. I had made that choice some years earlier, around the time Eugene had been killed, and I remained unshaken in my selection. I knew, in the summer of 1920, that my decision to love her had been made much earlier, but I had not recognised that decision and its significance until then. At first, I was drawn to her by her kindness, by her refusal to comment on my scar and by her own sadness. Perhaps it was also because of my need to fill a gap in my horizon, which my parents had occupied until I was about twelve.

Children need adults; they are like fence-posts on the edge of the field that is your life. They serve the dual purpose of keeping you from straying onto the road unsupervised, and at the same time keep the world at large from trespassing into the field. The need to focus my attention on someone bigger was always there, and just at the precise moment when Eugene might have relieved my parents at their posts, that change of guard was rendered impossible by a German bullet. When I could no longer accept my parents' boundaries or their rules, I switched my attention to someone else. Miss Pleyben would become as constant in my life and on my horizon as they had been, and as Eugene should have been, but now could not be. My brother formed part of the soil in northern France, and was well beyond anything I could see ahead of me.

Vivienne Pleyben was much more than just my geography teacher. She had nursed me through four or five years with encouraging smiles and precious eye contact. She had stood at the front of my universe, facing me and feeding me information and hope from tatty geography books written by dreamers in Paris. She had led me all around the world, from Venezuela to the Carpathians and to America, and back. We were like honeymooners each week, taking trips together. The rest of the class came with us, but they idled in museums, while we ate in expensive restaurants and stole moments together at fountains in secluded squares in Lisbon and Cairo. We visited the Pyramids and Australia, and were always back by four in the afternoon. I owed her so much, so very much.

"Aragon, move your arse," Charles Ferrier said, as he edged me over on the wooden bench outside the science

34

laboratory, one day at break time. The sun poured into the schoolyard through a gap created by the spire of the church and the slant of an escarpment halfway into the Dentelles. I eased myself over a little, and he ripped an apple in two with his inky hands and offered me a portion. I accepted it.

"I thought the priest was going to hit me last week, when I said that about the nuns at Prebayon."

"So did everyone else."

"Well, he wouldn't have done it twice."

"What would you have done? Would you have hit him back?"

The bigger boy thought for a few seconds, and then bit into the apple and spoke with his mouth full.

"I don't know, Aragon, I really don't."

I was heartened by his answer. I would have been disappointed if he'd told me that he'd been hoping for the opportunity to take a swipe at the priest. That was not the spirit of the silent revolution taking place in the graduating class in the lycée that summer. A fly hummed around a fragment of apple that had been sprayed from Ferrier's mouth as he spoke. The white mushy pulp lay on the lath of wood between us. Suddenly, Ferrier's massive right hand swooped down on the scene and caught the fly as it attempted to leave its treasure trove. Ferrier kept his fist closed for an instant and then opened it slowly and deliberately. The fly was thoroughly intact and alive. It delayed for a moment in the open hand before flying away. Perhaps it was dazed by the event, or maybe it knew Ferrier meant it no harm. Both Ferrier and the fly went up in my estimation.

Miss Pleyben walked by, visible for a moment inside one of the windows in the school. I felt warm inside, and the beginnings of an erection stirred in my grey flannel trousers. It didn't take much nowadays. I wondered if Ferrier noticed. I was almost certain he hadn't. I imagined that the fly would not have survived long if he'd remained on the palm of Ferrier's hand overnight. It was hot in every way imaginable that

June and I knew that things were changing. I thought of Yves Couderc and wondered if he were watching me.

GEOGRAPHY WAS the last class on Friday afternoons. Outside the classroom window, the trees in the schoolyard were as still as monuments in the relentless heat. On this Friday, Miss Pleyben made an announcement. "The geography projects have to be submitted by the thirteenth of June, ladies and gentlemen. There will be no exceptions because the judging meeting takes place three days later. This is the final chance that the members of this class have to win the geography prize."

The prize referred to an annual competition. The winner was chosen from among all the pupils in the school. Two teachers accompanied the victor to Avignon and the prize was, in effect, a short holiday there. The money to pay for the trip was provided by a gift made to the school two or three decades earlier. I hadn't a hope of winning really, but we were all entitled to dream.

Outside, over the school wall, I saw the top of someone's head walking in the direction of the village square. I was almost certain it was my father. We had barely spoken in the previous two weeks. The uncomfortable calm of argument lay between us since the day he'd denounced Algerians. We'd passed in the corridor outside our rooms from time to time, and shared the table at mealtimes. I had perfected the art of arriving late or excusing myself early, so that the long silences that usually preceded his outbursts didn't have a chance to materialise. I knew that a confrontation with him could end in violence, and I feared that.

The current state of affairs suited me, although I was unsure as to how long I could keep the tactic going. At any rate, it bridged the time between now and the end of the school year to a certain extent. That could only be good. I dreaded the looming vacation, as it would be my last, and also because of the inevitable life choice that lay within its confines. August would be the final month of whatever bit of my childhood I still had to live out. I did not know what I should or could do next, and in a way, the fear of that unknown was a kind of comfort, as it postponed the decision even further.

In a recent conversation, while he washed his massive hands in the stone trough outside the woodshed at Montmirail, George suggested that I should become a doctor.

"I don't think I'd be able to help people when they get sick."

"Why not?"

"I don't know. I think you have to be able to face sickness and death and not get worried by it."

George laughed. "I'm sure everybody thinks that before they study medicine at university. That's what they teach you, that's why they have to study for so long."

"I don't know, George. Maybe. It depends how I get on in the exams at the end of July."

"You'll be fine, Christian. You'll be just fine."

I did not want to be a doctor. The truth was that the only people I'd ever wanted to cure, Couderc and Eugene, were so far beyond the reach of any doctor now that I felt no real purpose could be served by my becoming one. Allied to this, of course, was the reality that no matter what I wanted to study or where I wanted to go, my father stood in my way, insisting that I should take over the vineyard. That meant beginning as soon as I graduated from school.

Eugene had always represented a barrier between my father and myself, soaking up my father's goodwill and my own misgivings, being everything to both of us. If Eugene were still alive, my relationship with my father might not have been much better, but it would certainly have been cushioned by Eugene's presence. Of necessity, Eugene's death had drawn our family in on itself in a way which would otherwise have been avoided. My mother lived in her Breton imagination for the most part, and only emerged to referee from time to time . . .

I was unsure whether it was losing sight of the bobbing head or hearing my name called that revived me first from my thoughts.

"Christian Aragon, are you with us today?" I looked up and Miss Pleyben's voice surrounded me like a breeze.

"Yes. Yes, Miss?"

"Welcome back, Christian. I was saying that you're the only one who has not yet told me the subject of your project."

"Well, Miss, I—"

"I know you've probably begun it already, but I need to submit the title with your name in order to get your exam number. See me after class, please."

"Yes, Miss."

I was being chosen to speak to her on my own. I couldn't believe it. It was like in my dreams when I could fly; I could go anywhere I wanted. And now, although my excuse for being where I wanted was perfunctory and practical, the sensations it provoked in my head and my heart were ethereal and magical. I drifted out of the classroom window until the bell rang in the corridor and the sharp mayhem of exiting classmates had left us alone. Miss Pleyben and I.

Her crimson blouse reminded me of the colour of knights' blood in storybooks. Her hair was tied back in a plait which became visible whenever she moved, and it shadowed behind her like a glimpse of someone else. I traced the outline of her body with my eyes and half hoped she would notice. If only she would take offence, then she could at least know some of my feelings, however inappropriately the information might convey itself. I thought of Pierre of Provence and Princess Maguelone of Naples. They had exchanged wedding rings in this small village, but I had nothing to offer in such an exchange. I felt at once wounded and breathless, waiting for her voice to begin again. She finished marking the roll-book, while I sat alone in the fourth row of the geography classroom, surrounded by maps of the world and charts outlining the decline of ore production in the Alsace-Lorraine region.

"Christian. Thank you for remaining behind." Miss Pleyben closed the roll-book gently and set it to one side on her desk.

"Yes, Miss," I answered, in a voice which did not sound familiar to me.

"You haven't selected a project yet, have you?" She smiled and her eyes were at once both accusing and forgiving.

"No, Miss," I answered. "You see, I was—"

She raised an index finger to stop me before I had a chance to tell lies. "There is no need to explain. I have been thinking about you for a while now, Christian."

I could feel myself blushing.

"This is a subject you can excel at if you put your mind to it."

I did not speak, because there was no need. I nodded my head.

"I have no doubt but that you have what it takes to win this trip to Avignon." Again I nodded.

"Are you prepared to sacrifice some spare time to give this project the effort required?" She spoke quietly while her eyes looked directly into mine. Then, she picked up an orange pencil from the desk with her right hand, and whether as a gesture of impatience or something more, slid it between her lips and waited for my response. I felt like I was going to explode inside and I took some short breaths before replying.

"Yes, Miss. I'm prepared to sacrifice . . ." I couldn't think of a suitable noun to tag onto the verb, so my voice trailed away.

Miss Pleyben got up from her chair, and came around to the other side of the desk and sat on it. She motioned for me

39

to come forward and handed me some pages folded in on each other. One of her legs dangled in the air while the other foot was on the floor. From between her legs, the corner of the desk pointed out at me like an accusation and a taunt. It was where I wanted to be. I noticed that my hands were shaking as I took the material from her.

"These are just a few suggestions for the project, but you really need to begin working on this immediately," she said.

I became aware of my own body as something almost alien, and I sought out her eyes for a sign of approval or rejection.

"Yes, Miss. Thank you, Miss," I murmured, as I made my way to the door. I glanced down the list and decided to choose "Reafforestation in the Alps." On my way home, I noticed my grey trousers were stained with adulthood.

Chapter Four

There is a legend about the origin of the name, Montmirail—
or the 'mountain of the mirror.' I have heard this story a
thousand times, but I will only tell it to you once, so that
you may know it forever. A viper lived in a well in Gigondas
hundreds of years ago. This snake was evil and constituted a
danger to the entire village. Anybody who looked directly at
the serpent died immediately. As a result, many of the beautiful girls in the village who came to admire their reflection
in the water met with a hastier end than they might otherwise have expected. It is surprising that some of the girls did
not have a similar effect on the viper since, of course, in any
large group there will undoubtedly be some swine as well as
pearls! Anyway, one day, a knight wearing a suit of armour
came along and had the idea of holding a mirror up to the
viper. The viper died and the mountain was named.

I never know whether or not to believe in such things. As
with the story of the wedding-ring exchange, the legend of
the Mirror Mountain lodged in my head early on in my life
and stayed there. It was an old story from nearby, and that
too is probably why I stored it in my internal archive. When
I became old enough to have a family of my own, I supposed
that would be the time to hand on these stories. Whether
or not I believed them shouldn't matter much. But as the
summer of 1920 approached, it was something deeper than
old stories and future children that stirred me to find my
own story, my own page in whatever novel God writes. I
hadn't held a rifle in my hands at Verdun in the shadow of
Fort Douaumont. I hadn't died for France. Nor was I fes-
tering inside with dreams of the *Medaille d'Or*. I was just a

boy trying to become a man. I was sixteen-and-a-half years old with a bundle of hormones and a geography project that was almost finished.

Miss Pleyben lived in a small house on the edge of the village, just below the mountains. Nighttime on the next market day found me making my way past the fever hospice to the stubborn track which led to her isolated home. I was not myself that evening. Please do not misunderstand me when I say that. I don't mean that I am distancing myself from my actions because of shame or guilt. Quite the contrary. In fact, I am in awe of the soul which uses my body to chase dreams and ghosts from time to time. I merely give credit where due rather than dare to believe that I, Christian Aragon, could be the architect of these soulful chases.

In 1890 or 1891, the last of the wolves around Gigondas disappeared. I remember my grandfather telling me about hunting them in the early spring. In the trees above her house, at the raw edge of the hills, these creatures had hidden and made dawn raids from there on the *grangeons* and chicken-runs in the village, snatching food for themselves and their young. I myself was only a cub on that evening, but I knew what I wanted to capture—an unguarded glimpse of the woman I loved. I left the village behind me as I climbed the track, keeping out of the line of sight of the windows at the front of the house. A cypress grove to the rear of the house invited me to sit and stare. Was I a wolf? Did I come to take something which did not belong to me? I like to think not, but who can be sure what drives the heart to propel the body into certain situations? What fluid drips slowly from the brain to the feet and makes you walk one way and not another? There is an irresponsibility in youth that is at once restrictive and liberating. It enchants and disappoints all in a moment and leaves you in breathless hope of more.

Miss Pleyben lived alone, and I wondered if she ever missed her husband. Stephane Pleyben was an awkward, awful man who had barged his way into her life and then out of it again. It was widely believed that he'd left to avoid fighting the Germans. He'd sniffed the gunsmoke from the newspapers and fled. By the time Eugene had volunteered to fight, that coward had been gone six months. The only trace of his absence had been the gradual emergence of Vivienne into our world with smiles and laughs, instead of the makeup she'd used before to hide her marriage from the rest of mankind. In deference to the horror of her union, she was always called 'Miss' instead of 'Madame.'

A gas lamp flickered on for a moment and then moved to another room. The evening was reeling in the night and soon it would be time for the cicadas to begin their song. I sat on a tuft of grass behind an old tree, and from time to time saw her through the window going about her chores. She washed a single plate and dried it with a patterned cloth, then sat at the kitchen table with a small glass of something in her right hand. I watched as she sipped from it slowly. The mountains behind us grew dark and somehow more precise in outline, until at last the sun sank behind Orange and the day was over. I could see lights in the village below, and from down there too the sound of a cart on the Carpentras Road floated up and into the leaves above me.

When it was totally dark I moved forward, and the wolf in me used the advantage of night to advance on my quarry. Where there was light within the house, I knew I could get closer and closer and still not be seen. So I crept on my hands and knees until I came to the final portion of my cover, where the edge of the light from within met the grass. At this point, the width of a fingernail separated invisibility from detection. Through the glass I could see her bedroom. There was a vivid red blanket on the bed that seemed to gather the room around itself like a clown or a corpse might. On a stand in the farthest corner, a ewer and a china

43

basin cast an odd combined shadow on the wallpaper whose design I could not make out. The lamp must have been to the right of the window on a chair or table judging from the direction of the light. I had not seen Miss Pleyben for a while now and assumed she must be in the front room, reading or correcting assignments. But since she'd lit a lamp in the bedroom, I suspected that she intended to enter and use that room soon.

All of a sudden, the back door opened and a torrent of light spilled onto the grass. I heard a noise in the kitchen and knew that if she emerged holding a lamp then I would certainly be seen. Perhaps I already had been. I felt myself redden. I contemplated making a run for it, but eventually decided to wait and let the light determine whether I was still safe. Vivienne Pleyben stepped out the back door and onto a narrow patch of gravel. I heard the rustle of her clothes, and then she sighed audibly and stood for a moment. The light had been ushered out in one direction and that was probably because the door was half-open. For an instant she looked to her right, and I felt so sure that she must see me that I almost spoke. She turned away and walked into the darkness. I heard another door and then I knew—she'd emerged to use the outhouse. I took three steps backwards and lay down on the grass. I waited.

Sometime later I was conscious of waking, although I had no recollection whatsoever of nodding off. It was strange and dry under me. The grass pushed against my skin in the gap between my trousers and shirt which exposed my stomach. The door was closed now and there was light only in the bedroom. Just as I was about to step forward and dare the lamplight, Miss Pleyben moved into the space between the window and the bed. It was like a newsreel we'd seen once in the village hall, all light and shade and movement that seemed unnatural in its speed.

She was almost naked, wearing only a blue striped, unbuttoned chemise. I could feel my heart quicken. I know you will probably imagine that other parts of me were stirred too, and that desire or lust was my primary reaction, but I must tell you that you are wrong. My immediate feeling was a sense of overwhelming privilege that my time and hers had collided there, at that place and in that way. I cannot tell you how much my heart was bursting with pride and happiness at seeing her. Clothed or naked, day or night, for one minute or for a century, it was all the same to me. It mattered not a wisp of smoke or a dead leaf what the circumstances were that brought us to any shared time. I only cared that we were there, each alone and yet somehow together. Sure, I wanted her in other ways. Of course, I thought the thoughts of teenage boys at the sight of beautiful women. But if I could not have seen her ever again, apart from that moment through her window, my disappointment could not have dented my joy. I loved her unconditionally. That kind of love is well used to making do with morsels and night-time glimpses, when breakfast and daylight are not yet possible.

What did you expect of me there, in the darkness, with my heart's desire only paces away and almost entirely bared to me? Do you think that I will tell you that some sad eventuality of self-pleasure and peeping combined to complete my hunt? Do you attend on notice of youth and desire and await my confession? I can confess only this to you: that when pure skin and untainted lips and unfractured beauty stood at the window oblivious to my presence, then I stood still and watched and felt my heart seep out onto the space between us, and prayed for the moment to last forever. I wanted to be pure too, and I wanted to be able to say that if a passerby had seen me, he or she would have thought me proper and full of happiness; a little unusually situated perhaps, but courteous and mannered in the unknowing sight of the object of all of my love. I must tell you that although I wanted my geography teacher, in the way that most men inevitably want women, I was beyond contented with my glimpse into her life. Had she been fully clothed, I would not have found her any less desirable. I ached and I wanted her, but I did not cheapen my chase, nor could I have prized my quarry any more. If you have ever truly loved, you will know that I am honest in all these matters.

When the lamp had been dimmed and the curtains drawn against the night, I watched her shadow slow to sleep and made my way back down the hill to my own bed.

The head teacher in the school, Monsieur Arsac, interrupted our class when we were in the middle of trying to solve some awful math problem in late June.

"Pardon me, but may I have your attention please?" He tapped his spectacles on the blackboard.

We were delighted by this distraction from algebra.

"The winner of the geography project prize for 1920 is—" He paused, and we all imagined it might be us in the seconds before the announcement would shatter those pretensions. "—Christian Aragon!" Monsieur Arsac spoke my name with as much surprise as I felt, and everyone else must have been feeling. There was a short burst of applause and then some cheers from Beaumet and Ferrier.

"Avignon?" my father sneered, while we stood together in the courtyard some days later. "What do you need to go there for? To see the Pope? I don't know what use geography or history can be to a boy like you. This place and the future are what should concern you, not anything else."

"It's a wonderful achievement, it really is," my mother said, with a frightened smile. "It's great that you've won this prize."

"What use is a stupid bloody prize?" he shouted.

I immediately thought about the *Medaille d'Or*.

"It's only for two nights, Robert. It will be good for him," she said.

"He's not going," my father announced as he left the room, slamming the door behind him like a spoiled child.

46

"What could you have learned in Avignon which would have helped you make good wine here for the next thirty years?" my father asked a couple of days later, as we found ourselves in the courtyard once again.

I didn't reply; although it was a rhetorical question, I knew that some response was demanded. Expected. I knew that he wanted me to be cowed and to agree, but I sensed too that his tone sought to provoke. If my father could coax an argument out of me, it might be the drip before the deluge to allow the war about loyalty, family business, inheritance, and the obsolescence of dreams to begin even before the school term ended. I had learned from experience that predictability is a great weakness; so I ignored the remark, and pretended I had not even heard it by shouting at George as he emerged from the cellar.

"Are you going to Sablet?" I asked him—though I knew he wasn't.

"Are you listening to me?" my father snapped.

"Yes," I said, lazily.

"Then what did I say to you a moment ago?" His eyes cranked up the furnace in his face and he stood straight, moving closer to maximise the confrontation.

"You asked if I was listening to you, Papa." I could see his rage beginning. He spoke slowly and deliberately through his teeth. "Before that."

"I have no idea. I thought you were talking to yourself, so I blocked it out to give you some privacy." I smiled as I spoke.

BANG. My father's fist connected with the side of my face. I expected my immediate response would be to cry, but something stopped me. I managed to stay on my feet and keep my hands at my side.

"No wonder we won the war," I said. "Imagine how much sooner the Germans would have given up if *you'd* gone to the front instead of Eugene."

For an instant I thought he was going to hit me again, but just then we both sensed George's proximity to the courtyard, and the creak of a door gave away my mother's presence in the scullery at the rear of the house. My father started to speak, but I didn't want to give him the opportunity to explain himself. I turned my back on him and walked towards the house. I listened for his footsteps or the shouts that would be the sign of an attempt by him to retake the initiative, but none came.

My hands were shaking and my left leg was shivering when I reached the safety of my own room. I lay on the floor rather than the bed, thinking that to relax would mean being off-guard before it was safe. My father had not struck me for some years now, and this was the first time I could have retaliated as a young man and perhaps even done some damage. I couldn't believe that I'd resisted. I would store up the event until I needed strength against him. I felt that the war had begun, but I was at a loss to understand exactly how it would be fought. Realizing that until this moment I had never believed I could win, somehow I knew then—as the raised voices of my parents replaying the episode in the kitchen reverberated in my ears through the floorboards— that I must not allow myself to lose. I did not want this inheritance. I wanted to make my own mistakes and my own life.

Families are conspiracies of convenience, where abnormal behaviour sometimes steals the show. I had begun years earlier to question the validity of the inheritance of duty and obligation. What is it about families that blinds us to the behaviour of certain members, when we would counsel friends or strangers to leave their families if they told us of their own, similar experiences? It cannot be love, because when that dies out, we would be free again. Perhaps it is obligation, but you would think that criticism of the behaviour would negate any feelings approximating loyalty. The only other possibility is fear. I was frightened, but I wanted to fight back. I felt for my scar, and for the first time ever, could not put my finger on it immediately. Had it healed? No. But to me at that time it was certainly less noticeable.

"VILE INFLUENCES will try to insinuate themselves into the life of the young person. These forces may take many forms, such as conversations about Free Will, shared stories, or printed material of a lewd or bawdy nature. As a chameleon changes itself to suit its environment, so too do these forces adapt to spread their tentacles into the virgin mind and body. Unless these invasions are repelled, they will inexorably lead to secret acts of self-abuse."

Father Leterrier was tired, but still he preached on about Holy Purity. "It cannot be overstressed that this is the point in one's life where choices will have eternal and irreparable consequences."

Although it was warm outside, the classroom was not particularly hot that afternoon. But Fr. Leterrier's classes were now overheating in an entirely different way. The good priest wiped his brow with a handkerchief and made his way to the window. He opened it out as far as it would go. Someone outside will hear him now, I thought; and as if struck by a similar concern, he went back and closed it halfway. Ferrier sat to my left, picking his nose, using an open copybook as cover for this feast. The class seemed fragmented that afternoon, and despite the explicit nature of the teaching matter, no one seemed to be interested in upsetting the priest or provoking him into an argument. I cannot say how it came about, but it coincided with the warning that:

"Because of woman's role in God's holy design, a higher degree of delicacy and refinement is expected from her. Nowhere is this more evident than in matters of purity."

While those words were being spoken, there was a general sense of disapproval at the sentiment, although I assure you no sound came from the class. No human sound, that is. It began in the background of everyone's hearing, but gradually was forced forward as all other sounds fell silent except for it and the excited tones of Fr. Leterrier. It was a creak.

"Now, once a girl begins to lose her self-respect, to make herself cheap, to lower the standard of maidenly refinement, her capacity for good vanishes."

Creak. Creak. Creak-creak-creak-creak-creak . . . .

The voice stopped and suddenly the sound was all alone. Then I heard Abel Beaumet giggle; and Michel Darlan, who was sitting in front of me, turned and looked past me. I turned too. *Creak, creak.*

In the single desk at the rear of the class, Elise Morel sat with her eyes closed and her head tilted forward. *Creak, creak,* her desk squealed, as it rocked gently back and forth. The close concentration on her face was almost divine. Her arms pointed away down at the floor. Somewhere, in between, her hands were out of view, and she rocked back and forth in ecstasy, her face framed in passionate pleasure. A mixture of shock and delight descended over the entire class.

We all seemed to turn our eyes to Fr. Leterrier, waiting for his reaction. His eyes were like saucers: a strange mixture of blue bloodshot fury and frustration. He put down his pen on the desk beside him, and walked three paces into the centre of the middle aisle. *Creak.* Like a timid man faced with violence, he breathed heavily and rapidly until he forced his words out in a hoarse whisper and launched them at the back wall. *Creak, creak.*

"Mmmiss Morel?" He hissed hesitantly.

The creaks increased in frequency and then stopped abruptly. Elise's eyes flicked open, as if awakened from only a moment's closure.

"Yes, Father?" she said, in a tone which was neither embarrassed nor brazen.

"What are you *doing*, Miss Morel?" I could see that he instantly regretted asking the question and wished he'd simply asked her to stop or leave. Anything—except invite an explanation.

"Doing, Father? Surely you know only too well what I'm doing?"

"I do not, Miss Morel. I do not." His voice got stronger and louder, but he retreated like an exorcist who has taken on too big a task.

Slowly and deliberately, Elise Morel licked her lips provocatively, and began to raise her arms. As she breathed in, her breasts swelled in her blouse. The class and the priest were transfixed and no one knew what to expect. Her wrists, then her hands, came into view and she exhaled. Elise Morel raised them the last couple of inches, and then opened her cupped hands to the world like a conjurer. In her palms, a set of rosary beads coiled in repose like a sleeping viper.

"Praying to Our Lady for maidenly refinement, Father," she announced.

The bell rang for the end of the class and our innocence.

CHAPTER FIVE

"Do you know how Petrarch described this city?" Miss Pleyben asked, as we arrived through the gate in the wall onto Cours Jean-Jaurès, and my feet met Avignon.

"No, Miss."

"'A sewer where all the filth of the universe has gathered,' Christian. That's what Petrarch made of it." She raised her hands, and in a gesture, presented the city to me.

"Why did he say that, Miss?"

"Because it was true, I suppose." She smiled as she spoke. "Do you know when Petrarch made that remark?"

I was being tested on the short history of Avignon she'd given me one afternoon the week before our trip. I had studied it minutely.

"After the Black Death in 1348?"

She smiled again, but this time I felt that the smile was for me.

"Absolutely right, Christian. When criminals and heretics gathered here to hide in the shadow of the Papacy. When plague followed famine, and the scent of death was the first thing a newborn baby knew."

"But that was hundreds of years ago, Miss. Avignon is not like that now. Is it?"

"I hope not, Christian. But we shall find out."

It was another world, this blue and grey town, rising up like a brick menace over the river Rhône. As we walked side by side in the street, people sometimes looked at us. I wondered what they thought about. Outside the Palais du Roure, we stopped for a few minutes to catch our breath. A tiny fountain played into the afternoon air like a juggler.

To the right, on the edge of a pillar with iron gates, a small drinking spout in the shape of a lion watered us until we were full. I felt the water splash onto my shirt and trousers, and then I gulped and gulped; water and air, air and water, until my stomach hurt and I stopped. All this time, Miss Pleyben watched me and I felt her eyes on my shirt, my head, and on the splashes of water that jumped past me onto the pavement. I drank longer than was prudent, but that was because I loved the attention. I craved the sensation of being watched, but apparently being unaware of it. It reminded me of my night outside her house weeks earlier.

"That's enough, leave some for me."

Her voice revived me. I lifted my head and let the water slow down as my hand released the head of the lion. I felt her behind me as I turned, and I wished we were naked and alone. She looked as though she was going to scold me, but then she shrugged her shoulders and ruffled my hair with her hands. For an instant I almost tried to kiss her, but held myself back. It was as though a part of me knew more about all of this than I really did, and I bided my time without knowing why.

We walked on together into the crowds of people going the other way. As we did so, I felt the sun on my shoulders pushing me up the street. The dark corners of bright shops seemed to come alive and taunt the day through vitrines, as though our passing by had disturbed them into life. Here, a new dress leaned out to see, and over there the enticing aroma of baking drew us deliberately nearer to one side of the street.

"Are you alright, Christian?" Miss Pleyben asked, as we took the left turn just before the Place du Palais and entered the Rue de la Balance.

"Yes, Miss," I replied, without really considering her question. We had arrived at our lodgings; the tiny Hotel St. Sauveur. As we stood together on the front step, she turned to me and spoke for the first time as if we might have been the same age.

"Please call me Vivienne. 'Miss' is too formal I think. We only have two days here and then we'll be back to the school again; but while we're here, let's address each other as friends. Okay?"

"Okay." This time I'd heard the question and hoped I was beginning to understand.

The concierge was a small crooked man with an enormous straight nose. His eyebrows almost met in the centre of his forehead, but some inscrutable reticence kept them apart. He looked at our two small bags with derision and then asked, slyly, "Will your luggage be arriving later?"

Miss Pleyben—Vivienne—cut him in two with a swish of her hand and replied, "We were advised to travel as lightly as possible because of the reputation of Avignon for thieves." She winked at me.

The little man was put in his place and took our bags in his old rigid hands and led the way to our rooms at the top of the house. Miss Pleyben had told me on the train from Orange to Avignon that Herve Duchen, who taught the fifth-years, and was supposed to accompany us on the trip, had travelled to Paris instead. I was surprised when she added that he'd gone to see his mistress in the Boulevard St. Jacques, and that we were to cover for him. I was delighted we were going to be alone.

Of course, I was thrilled about having her all to myself, but there was something more. I think that it was at this point exactly that I began to entertain the faintest of possible hopes, namely, that she might have some sort of feeling for me.

My room was simple: bed, chair, table, and a tiny wardrobe that had a door that was glued shut so you couldn't use it anyway. I unpacked in less than half a minute, and I put the clean pair of trousers my mother had packed over the back of the chair. I went to the window and looked out onto the

Rue de la Balance. The buzz of conversations drifted up from the street, but fragmented into air and incomprehensibility by the time it reached me. I watched a boy with a hoop chase it down the street. I laughed to myself as it passed perfectly through the gap between one customer entering and another leaving a clothing shop. It was late in the afternoon now and my stomach growled for food. I left the window open and sat on the bed. A small knock on the door announced Vivienne's arrival.

"May I come in?" she asked, opening the door, but not enough to see into the room.

"Sure," I answered. My heart began to beat faster and we met in the mirror on the wardrobe before we met, if you know what I mean.

"I don't know about you, but I'm hungry," she said.

"Me too, Vivienne." There, I'd said it, used her name; and now I moved closer to her world and it hadn't taken much courage, not much courage at all. She'd given me that key and I'd used it. Turned the lock and opened the door. I arrested my thoughts and followed her along the corridor and then down the stairs. The man with the huge nose barely looked up from the desk as we passed, and he said nothing. We were supposed to leave our room keys with him if we went out. But we didn't. We stepped out into Avignon.

"Let's go left," she suggested.

I nodded, and we marched with purpose back towards the Place de L'Horloge. I brushed past people who all seemed to be somehow smaller and lighter than myself. We side-stepped a large pile of boxes outside a hat shop. As we rejoined on the other side—I cannot say at whose instigation it occurred—we were holding hands and saying nothing, and looking for a restaurant. It is difficult for me to remember now what we ate or where we sat. I can only really say that I enjoyed the meal without noticing it, and noticed an erection in my pants without enjoying it. She drank a little wine, and I consumed glass after glass of water, hoping to distract my nether region into more ordinary use. She was beautiful. She wore a simple dress which revealed a mole on her right shoulder and hid most of her chest under a thin white-bordered collar. I did not know where to look most of the time, and whenever I did catch myself looking, it was at her warm face on my way back up from her breasts. She did not seem to mind, and she spoke gently and kindly to me of how we would visit the Palace of the Popes on the following day, and the Porte St. Dominique and the ramparts near Porte Magnanen. She urged me to be vigilant.

"Christian, you have only two days to enjoy this city, so keep your eyes open."

"I will," I promised. "I will."

She was calm and measured, fresh and lovely, and the words she spoke drifted over to me like butterflies crossing a meadow. I did not know whether I'd taken her hand or she mine. I was unsure if that was an accident or an indulgence. I was certainly in the dark as to whether what I should expect next was forgiveness for a mistake, or another tiny step on the road to intimacy. To be honest, I was completely confused. If I'd been out of line, she gave no indication of upset or reproach. On that afternoon, I wanted to overturn the table and kiss her while the stuffy old men and women in the restaurant looked on.

After dinner, we walked for hours around the streets of that great city. I took in the scenes and sounds and recall, in the most vivid detail, the facade on the Hotel des Mônnaies, with its spitting lions disgorging fruit and flowers in stone. The eagles and dragons of the Borghese family were flattened by the rain in places, and scorched by the sun almost in their entirety. I was more acutely aware of Vivienne, however, and we strolled together down the lucky streets of Avignon. We held hands, and I loosened my grip from time to time, inviting her to break away and tell me I'd been mistaken. She did not tell me that I had been mistaken. She pulled me closer to her as we walked, and as we did, our arms too were as close as our clothes would allow. The wrists of my shirt-sleeves were damp with anticipation and I smiled at complete strangers, feeling for the first time ever that I belonged. I thought *about* her. I closed my eyes momentarily and I *saw* her inside my head, then I opened them again and I was *with* her. During class, for all of those years, I'd imagined myself in her company taking trips to faraway places. In my mind, we'd soared over the Mediterranean and had visited Africa and Peru and Japan together, while the rest of the class stared blankly at their books, or looked halfheartedly out of the window. But now we really *were* travelling together, and Avignon was as exotic as heaven or the moon.

We passed by cafés and heard laughter locked away. Then we were suddenly swept along by the people around us, and found ourselves at the west facade of the Church of St. Pierre. A statue of the Virgin Mary in the west porch of that church looked out at us; and for an instant I knew that I was in some way still a child, and also knew that I now wanted to advance beyond that point.

"I suppose *you're* a virgin, too?" she said with a laugh, as we turned away and let our feet lead us towards the Pont St. Bénezet.

I thought I would blush, but I didn't. Instead, something in me recalled Fr. Leterrier, and I replied, "I've become a little tired of Holy Purity lately."

Vivienne smiled and turned to face me and held me by both hands. "So have I."

It only took the slightest of touches, and we knew that the moment had arrived. A strand of hair fell onto the side of her face, and I pushed it back and behind her ear. She whispered something, it may have been my name, and we kissed. Her kiss was so soft and inviting, and tasted slightly of wine. I kissed her back. She was the first girl I'd ever really kissed—if you don't count the lady from the Metal for Munitions Association, who'd turned her lips to mine at the last moment as I went to kiss her goodbye on the cheek after

Eugene's funeral. I felt a warm chill shoot through my body, and I put my arms around her neck and kissed my geography teacher as well as I thought I knew how.

When we finished, she kissed me on the eyes and all over my face, stroked my cheek and said, "Oh, Christian, what has happened to our worlds that we are here?"

I had no idea what she meant, but I figured at least she wasn't mad at me or anything. We began to walk again.

"St. Bénezet was a shepherd who began to build this bridge in 1177 after divine inspiration even though—"

"Even though the people of Avignon mocked him." I finished her sentence from the notes on Avignon which she'd given me. Vivienne smiled, and for an instant we were teacher and pupil; but then our bodies hauled us back to the present where we were something altogether different.

In the middle of the bridge in Avignon lies the Chapel of St. Nicholas. It is an odd building split into two levels. The stone was cold to the touch, and through the open windows I heard the sound of the Rhône gushing south to the sea. An old lady carrying a basket of firewood passed us as we entered the chapel. She looked up at us as she went by, and in her eyes I sensed a disapproval that reminded me of my father. For an instant, I thought of my classmates: Ferrier, Beaumet, Elise Morel, Mathilde Bremond, Julie Saudrel. I knew all of their names, and they knew mine, but I could not really describe them as close friends. When I thought about it, George was more of a friend to me than they were. Couderc, in a way, had been the nearest I'd achieved to close contact with anyone, apart from Eugene. Eugene had been my hero long before he became one for France.

A drop of water fell from the ceiling of the chapel onto my head, and I stood where I was and looked up so as to try and catch the next one in my mouth. It struck me on the nose and I tasted it as it slid down my face. It was clear and pure and reminded me of the salt from my mother's tear I'd tasted in the cradle. I closed my eyes.

Vivienne must have been watching me because I heard her laugh. I kept my eyes closed and I felt the warm comfort of her breath on my face. Her lips closed in on mine and her strong tongue explored my mouth. I continued to keep my eyes shut and she kissed me deeply. I felt her hands release my shirt from inside my belt, and suddenly her flesh was against mine. She guided me slowly backwards into a corner at the end of the chapel aisle. I put my arms around her neck, but she gently lifted my right hand, linked her fingers in mine, and led my hand under the arm of her dress. I was unsure of what to do, but as she placed my hand against her breast, I felt her nipple harden. I caressed it and it grew in my fingers, and her whole body shook slightly as we manoeuvred ourselves against the cold wall.

Now I opened my eyes and hers were closed. We kissed and kissed and I felt like I was going to explode. A sound outside the chapel door startled both of us, and for an instant I expected Father Leterrier or the police or the woman with the basket to fling open the doors of the church and rebuke us. The moment passed as the sound faded, and Vivienne took me by the hand. We walked to the other side of the chapel. There, a confessional box guarded the right-hand aisle from the light through the stained-glass window of St. Bénezet and his sheep. She put a finger to her lips and opened the door in the centre which gave a tiny squeak. I saw the small seat with its velvet cover, and Vivienne pushed me ahead of her and I sat down and faced her. Quickly and effortlessly, she leaned over and undid my belt and buttons, and released my excitement from the confines of my mother's laundry. I wanted to speak, to ask what to do next, to say, 'Is it alright? Am I big enough? Are you okay?' But I could not.

Vivienne closed the door behind her and we were in complete darkness. For a long moment we were silent and I could hear the sound of my own breathing. I felt her hands about my face and then we kissed, and as our kiss ended I felt her ease a finger into my mouth, and we both licked it and each other. There was a small noise as she moved forward to position herself onto the seat with a knee on either side of me. Before I could really assimilate everything and figure out what to do next, she eased herself down onto me and I felt her wet, snug, other lips all around me. Her weight was nothing to me and she lifted herself up and down ever so slightly, while simultaneously edging her finger in and out of my mouth. My hands were under her now and I felt the smooth silkiness of the body I'd spied on only weeks earlier. We kissed again and she blew on my face and cooled me. I was dying to come inside her but was afraid.

I asked her in a breathless voice that seemed alien to me. "Is it okay? What about babies?"

She shushed me and whispered, "It's fine, Christian. Don't worry about that, it's all fine, just come, come inside me."

I moved her up and down more quickly now, pleasuring myself and losing all concerns in a feeling which welled up around me and consumed me inside-out. I could feel the tide rising within me now, and I thought for a split-second about how this time I wouldn't come inside one of the clean towels from the airing cupboard at home, and wouldn't have to think about pillowcases or sheets. Vivienne squeezed me with the muscles inside her, and it was as though she had an extra hand and it was bringing me to a climax. I'm in a confessional box and I haven't any sins to tell, I thought, as I exploded up inside her and a wave of wetness enveloped me deep inside my geography teacher in a cold stone chapel on a bridge. Criminals and heretics gathered here, and I hadn't thought about my scar all day. I was no longer a virgin; I'd been deflowered *"sur le Pont d'Avignon!"*

CHAPTER SIX

"Tell me about your husband."

"Stephane?"

"That was his name, wasn't it?"

Vivienne poked me in the ribs with her elbow as we lay in her bed that night, while a clock somewhere below us in the hotel chimed half-past one. The sound of unexpected rain through the balcony window was like a barrier between us and the world.

"You're a smart one, aren't you, Christian Aragon?"

"I don't really remember him, except that sometimes when you came to school, he would wait outside the gate until you'd gone inside."

"You saw that? You noticed it?"

"Sure. I was watching you once, and you turned to look at him and you waved, but he didn't wave back."

Her eyes narrowed and I saw tears form in the corners, just above the line of her cheek. "He never waved back, Christian. Not once, not one single time. He walked me to the school all right, he wanted to know where I was every minute of the day. He was the same when I got home in the afternoon: always wanting to know where I'd been after school, who I'd talked to, what we'd spoken about."

"Why?"

"So that he had control of my life, Christian. So that he knew where I was at every moment of the day."

"But why? Surely he had things to do himself, work, going out, hunting?"

She shook her head. "I'm afraid not. I was his obsession. He did nothing that didn't contribute to his control over me.

He became angry if anyone spoke to me in the street, and later, when we got home, he'd quiz me over and over again. 'Why did that person stop to talk? Are you having an affair with him?' Sometimes, he'd even wake me up in the middle of the night and turn on the lamp and begin his questions all over again. 'Why this? Why that?' "

I lay on my side with an arm propping up my chin, and watched the contours of her face as she spoke. I traced the line of her mouth with my free hand, and she pretended to snarl and try and bite it. Outside someone screamed, 'Salud,' from a high window somewhere down the street. A small candle flickered from the nightstand on her side of the bed, and its shadows giddied their way up and down the wall. I was sleepy and yet I dared not sleep, because the night held the promise of more love and learning. I hated to think of her husband and the way he had treated her. I hated to imagine her being touched, taken, violated by him.

"You wore a lot of makeup back then," I said, broaching the subject in a way that allowed her to reveal a little more of herself if she wanted.

"Yes, Christian," she said, petting my face with her hand. "I certainly did." As she finished speaking, she held my shoulder and pulled me towards her. In a short time, I was on top of her and she was guiding me inside herself for the third time that night. It was slow and uncomplicated, and fulfilled every dream I'd ever had about her and about how I wanted her.

In between, we talked and laughed and ate chocolates we'd bought on our way back to the hotel. We balanced the chocolates on each other's bare bodies and allowed those hors d'oeuvres to lead us on to other tastes of forbidden flesh and hidden fruit. I was sixteen but soon I'd be seventeen, and now and forever after I'd no longer be a boy or a child. She taught me the language of passion over the course of our stay in Avignon. I experienced the awesome heights of desire, expectation, appreciation, and fulfillment, which only wonderful, slow, unhurried, illicit love can bring when you're not quite seventeen.

Love? Yes, that was there too, in huge unquantifiable chunks as I pleasured and was pleasured by the only woman I'd ever loved or could imagine loving. I worshipped her body with mine and tasted every single part of her with the wild satisfaction of a gourmand in a chocolaterie. She encouraged me and praised me, and when my eagerness brought closure too early, she welcomed it and transformed my errors into heroics with the kindest of words and touches. She moulded me through those two nights into someone who could finally feel loved in return. We fused in the most intimate way imaginable, and each touch and whisper brought us closer and closer until I felt that I could slip into her life, unnoticed by the world, and remain there forever, as enthusiastic and as passionate and as adoring as if I were still only an admirer from afar.

"Why me?" I'd asked, in the course of our first night together.

"What do you mean?" Her face was close to mine. The scent of her made me dizzy.

"I mean, how come you're here with me and not, say, Ferrier or Beaumet? I mean, if they'd not finished their projects, would you be with one of them in Avignon instead?"

I knew from the silence that I'd hurt her. I didn't mean to, but I had. For a few seconds I thought she might get out of bed and leave me, but instead she explained and reassured me.

"I've been alone for some years now, Christian. But I've been lonely for much longer. You see me as what, a teacher in control? An adult with freedom to do as I please, go where I choose? I'm just another person, Christian. A little older than you perhaps, but a person nonetheless. I've been aching for so long to reach out to someone else, to have them reach out to me too. I need more in my life than I have, or I'll die of a broken heart. I'd have died long ago if I hadn't met you.

63

I've watched you from a distance and seen your struggle and your heartache. I know I should have waited until you'd left school, but I honestly didn't know whether anything would happen between us here in Avignon. Sure, I hoped it would, I can't deny that, but I don't know what I can say or do to make you know that you are the person I desire and need. Nobody else would have done, if that's what you're asking."

She held out her hand to me and we linked fingers and grew closer in every possible way. She answered my questions with an intimacy and a vulnerability that left me in no doubt as to the truth of the words she spoke. Later, she told me how repeated assaults by her husband had left her incapable of bearing children.

"You saved me from a beating by him once," she said, looking up at the ceiling as we lay side by side later that night.

"That time in the square?"

"You remember? You were such a child then, so young, so small. How could you recall such an event? How old were you? It must have been before the war."

"I don't know, nine or ten maybe. I'll never forget the look on his face."

"We had been arguing," she said.

"About what?"

"About nothing, everything, oh, I don't know, but I do remember how he was about to hit me and then he saw you standing nearby, watching, with your fists clenched."

"I don't recall that."

"Yes, yes, they were tiny clenched hands. Do you remember what you said to him?"

"I didn't speak to him. I think I just looked at him, that's all."

"No, no." She turned her face to mine and kissed me. "You told him that you would fight him if he found you a box to stand on."

"I don't remember that."

"I remember it, Christian. I think it was from that moment on that I began to care about you. You were the only person who ever stood up to Stephane and I will never forget that."

"Where is he now?" I asked, as we began to drift off to sleep.

"I don't know," she answered. "Wherever he is, I hope he's dead."

"I HAVE a confession to make," I said, as we ate breakfast in a café on the Rue Boisserin on our final morning in Avignon.

"Oh yes?" Vivienne looked up from her coffee and smirked playfully. "Are you happy enough to make your confession here, or would you feel more comfortable in the chapel of St. Nicholas?"

I felt myself blush, but only for a moment, and for a different reason than she thought. "No, I mean it, there's something I should tell you." I didn't want there to be any secrets between us, and I did not want to keep this one at all.

"So tell me," she invited, smiling in a warm way which complemented the day around us, which enveloped us in the scent of coffee.

"I—" It was hard to begin. "I went one evening to—"

"To where, Christian? Tell me." She put down her cup.

"To your house, I went to your house and—"

"Was I there? Did you knock? Why didn't I hear you?"

"Y-yes, yes, you were there," I stammered.

She reached across the table and took my hand. "Tell me," she said. "It's alright."

"I watched. I saw you clean a single plate. I monitored the shadows and lay in the grass. I saw you in a blue chemise, and I devoured every single moment of that evening while you went about your chores and then undressed and went to sleep."

"Did you want me? Did you desire the person you saw that night?" She asked the questions softly.

"Yes, yes I did. I wanted you, but also I knew then that I—"

"Yes?" she whispered.

"That I loved you." I told her straight out.

"Oh, Christian," she said. "How wild and kind and honest you are."

"You're not angry?"

"Angry? Oh God, no, Christian. I'm not angry. I'm flattered, I'm pleasantly surprised, I'm as wet as a waterfall and I'd love to have you, here and now, in this café, before I finish my coffee. I'm a lot of things because of what you've told me, but angry is definitely not one of them."

She was so beautiful and I still could not believe that I was with her.

"Who was it you saw, for the last time ever, outside the bakery in Gigondas?"

Her question came out of the blue as we looked at the murals later that morning in the Chambre de Cerf in the Palace of the Popes. I was engrossed in the fishing scene and was trying to make notes. I looked up and answered without thinking. "Yves Couderc."

"Oh," she said. "The boy who died of TB?"

"Yes."

"The boy who—"

I reached for my scar. "Who gave me this? Yes."

Together we backed away from the mural in silence, seeking a different view of the scene.

"How did you know I'd seen someone for the last time outside the bakery?"

"I too have a confession to make."

"What confession?"

"I heard you once in the Chapel of St. Cosme, talking to God."

"You were there? Why?"

"I was just passing by when I saw that the door was open. I hadn't been in a church for years, and so I thought

I'd visit when there was no one around. But there was someone there."

"You know, I thought I heard someone. But when I looked around, the place was empty."

"I hadn't been in a church since, not until . . ."

We both smiled and remembered.

"That's the first time I've been in a confession box in ages," I said with a grin.

"I hope your soul is clean now," she said.

I was glad that Vivienne had been the one who observed me in the chapel when I'd tried to resolve the whole thing about Couderc with God. I told her so.

"I'm glad too, Christian. I'm happy that for one moment I was allowed inside your heart. It made me realise how far I've drifted from God in my own life."

"You've been in my heart for a very long time," I said.

"Thank you, Christian."

THERE WAS an easy happiness between us and it was as though we'd been friends and lovers for years. I didn't want it to end. A newspaper boy stood on the street outside the Palace of the Popes. He sold copies of Le Quotidien du Midi with an arrogance that could only have been earned. I saw an advertisement on the back of a folded copy: VÉGÉTALINE; CHEAPER THAN BUTTER, LIGHTER ON YOUR STOMACH. KEEPS BETTER AND CAN BE USED FOR ALL KINDS OF COOKING.

I remembered that my mother had bought this product earlier in the year, just after Easter. She'd been trying to save money, after George had told my father that the foreman at Domaine Grapillon d'Or predicted a poor crop for that year. My father always knew better than everyone else, though.

"What's this?" he'd asked aggressively, holding up the glass dish with the yellow, oily substitute.

"It's Végétaline," my mother answered. "You'd hardly know, and anyway, Paulette Canchier says it's much cheaper."

Crash! My father dropped the dish onto the stone floor. It shattered and yet the centre of the dish stuck to the Végétaline, and my mother went down on her knees to pick up the pieces. A shard of glass cut the thumb of her left hand and it bled onto the floor.

"It's much more expensive than butter, Chérie," my father corrected, while my mother crawled about the room. "You see, we'll have to get a new dish now, and I suppose you'll be off to the doctor about that tiny cut as soon as you get the chance."

"Hey, Christian." I felt a pull on my arm whisk me back to Avignon. Vivienne dragged me playfully by the sleeve across the street, to a shop which sold candles and chocolate. It was a shop made for us. I looked at her from behind as she paid for the chocolates. I imagined being a ghost or spirit, and just gliding forward to envelop her like a stencil captures the outline of a figure on a page, and doesn't lift its head until the design is completed. For the first time since we'd made love and kissed and been together in Avignon, I began to think about the future. Not years ahead, but even the following day. How would it be back in Gigondas? Would we still be lovers? Would it be possible to carry on our relationship at all, under the watchful eye of its inhabitants? Everyone presented a possible obstacle to us, from the Mayor, Gustave Le Vay, to the children in the first class at the school.

Around us the air was heavy with people and summer. The clatter of commerce and the grinding turn of cartwheels on the stone streets had no appeal for me. I had begun to miss the sound of the cicadas in the afternoon and the high rustle of different shades of green leaves in the Mistral. The pitch and rush of that great wind in the trees sometimes sounded so loud on the grounds of Montmirail, that it drowned out my thoughts and tossed George's shouts of 'hello' to the Dentelles instead of over in my direction. Yes, these were the sounds of my village, but my father's wish—that I should never hear any other sounds—made me even surer that I was unlikely to stay in Gigondas after I left school.

I split an apple in two with my pocket knife and we ate without speaking, crunching our way to the train station. The nasty concierge with the long nose was nowhere to be seen as we left the Hotel St. Sauveur. I was sorry to leave the hotel behind because I knew that I was leaving a part of myself there too. Some awkward, inopportune portion of my childhood was trapped forever between the glued wardrobe doors and windows over the Rue de la Balance. I was out now, away from some shadow that had held me back.

"What will we do when we get to Gigondas?"

Her question surprised me, as I had expected to be the one to ask it.

"I don't know, Vivienne."

"You'll have to call me 'Miss Pleyben' again." She smiled. "That's certain at least."

"It's going to be strange, sitting in class and watching you and knowing that . . ."

"I know, Christian. It's going to be difficult for me too. But we will have to be careful."

"I know. I don't want you to get into any trouble at the school. I don't think they'd like it if—"

"No, they wouldn't. It's going to be difficult. People will be watching us anyway because we've been away. Make sure you say that Monsieur Duchen was with us."

"My father will be back from Paris tomorrow."

I shuddered to think of what would happen if he ever suspected anything. In a way, I almost hoped that he might find out. It would be another skirmish in the mountains before the confrontation on the battlefield proper. My mother had consented to my making this trip only because he'd be away on either side of it. I think that, in a sense, her defiance of his wishes in this manner accorded her a degree of independence. Perhaps, too, it was even a little retribution for things like the Végétaline incident or the emotional gulf between them, which was only bridged physically in the most base and thoughtless way. In the same expanse of Provençal landscape in which some people cultivated mulberry trees to nourish silk worms, the Aragon household stood its ground and maintained its place in the village through a mixture of tradition and obduracy. I was on my way back there now with some extra knowledge, and maybe even the strength to break away from what was expected.

"We must be very careful, Christian."

Vivienne spoke in a whisper as we stood on the platform of the station at Avignon, waiting for the train to Orange. I knew that she was right, but part of me wanted to take her hand and hold it up to the sun and the world and scream, "I love this woman." I knew that whatever lay ahead of us would not be easy or pleasant. We needed each other—that was clear to me at any rate. She, the abandoned wife alone in a village of parents and pupils, and me, the ungrateful scion of the oldest wine-producing family in the Rhône valley.

We'd made plans. I spooled recollections through my mind's eye, while we waited and watched the heat rise off the iron tracks that petered off to a point in the distance. I remembered our voices in the dark, what we'd vowed to each other in the cosy warmth of the hotel.

"Will you wait for me to grow up and be with you always?"

"Yes, yes I will, Christian. But when you're older you won't want an old lady like me."

"How old are you now?"

"Twenty-four."

"That's not old."

"Not even when you're only sixteen? Doesn't it seem very old?"

"No, you're young, you're like me; looking for someone to share your dreams with."

"Will you wait for me, Christian?"

"Forever, if I have to."

"I hope it won't be that long."

"I hope so, too."

The train made itself known to our ears before we sensed it in any other way. The mellow hum and buzz on the iron tracks was like a bee trapped in a demi-john. As it approached, we glanced at each other and Vivienne began to cry. She looked away from me when she knew that I was watching her.

"What is it, Vivienne?" I put my hand on her shoulder and turned her around so that we faced each other.

"Nothing, it's nothing. Really."

"I don't believe you."

"I'm crying because I'm happy, Christian. You've made me so happy."

"School finishes in three weeks," I said. "Then our lives can really begin."

I made myself a promise there and then on the platform that we *would* be together, forever. I knew that there would be obstacles no matter what I did or where I went. I remembered the fireworks the previous year on the feast of St. Cosme and St. Damien. I recalled her features in minute detail lit by the colours of the September sky. I'd buy coffee beans at the market in Seguret one day soon and bring her breakfast in bed. No one and nothing, not my father or the social etiquette of Gigondas or anyone or anything else, would stop the inexorable march of Christian Aragon towards his chosen destiny. I would be strong and tall and alone sometimes if I had to be. But I would take every single step on that path even if it meant forsaking the plans of men, gods or devils, to be with the woman I loved. I touched my scar with a sense of pride for the first time ever. I wished for the heat of battle and the sting and mark of steel to cross and cover my body, if necessary, in the burned insignia of passion and love.

As the train came to a halt, I pulled Vivienne to me and kissed her for the last time before she became Miss Pleyben again for a while. A figure in the carriage behind her back returned my gaze over her shoulder. I closed my eyes and took up my small bag from the railway platform.

"Oh, God," I said quietly. "It's Father Leterrier."

CHAPTER SEVEN

"Take off that uniform—you're not fit to polish the buttons on it," my father roared. It was the day after the telegram had arrived, telling our family of Eugene's death. I undid the tunic and took it off, folding it awkwardly before laying it on top of the trunk where I'd found it. My father stood in the doorway of the bedroom.

"And the rest of it," he ordered. I stepped out of the trousers, with their blue stripes down each leg. As I turned to place them on top of the tunic, I heard the slap of his leather belt being whipped from around his waist. I raised my arm instinctively to protect my face, but was a fraction too late. The double force of the leather struck me before my hand could shield my cheek, and the clout knocked me to the ground. The blows began to rain down on my bare torso, my arms, my legs, and on the back of my head, as I sat in a huddle trying to keep the belt away from my face. I do not know how long the beating continued, but it seemed that no part of my flesh escaped my father's grief and wrath on that February afternoon in Gigondas. At one stage I began to lose consciousness, and felt my head spin as my skin burned from the weals and welts. The musty smell of my brother's room reminded me that I was now an only child.

"Robert," my mother screamed, from the same spot in the doorway from which he had ordered me to undress. "Stop it! Stop it!"

It was the last beating I received from him, apart from that punch in the face in the courtyard in Montmirail during my last days there, when I'd deliberately misunderstood what he'd said. I recalled frequently how he'd not uttered a single word during my beating over the uniform, and how neither of us had spoken of it afterwards.

"Your father is very sad about Eugene." My mother made a half-hearted excuse for him as she treated my injuries with ointment.

"So am I," I whispered, beneath my crying. "So am I."

THE ALGERIAN man who'd come to work at Domaine de la Mavette had a kind face. He saluted me in the Place de la Fontaine on the Wednesday after I'd returned from Avignon. This act of kindness and courtesy was in contrast to the reception which had greeted his own arrival in certain parts of the village. I understood from local gossip that someone had taken a swing at him when they'd met him on the road to Les Florets. By all accounts, he'd been more than able to look after himself, and the assailant had wound up in a ditch. I couldn't understand this type of antipathy towards a man because of the colour of his skin. My father, of course, had no such difficulties.

I'd saluted the Algerian in return at the fountain. To me, he was a better man than my father would ever be, as I recalled his latest barrage of bigoted remarks during a recent dinner-table conversation.

"Parasites, that's what they are. God-fearing Frenchmen work their hands off to the wrist and these half-breeds come to take their jobs and their land. What next, I wonder? Mixed marriages?"

"I suppose they just have different traditions," I posited in response.

"Traditions? What traditions?" My father sneered. "They breed camels, eat sand, and sit out in the sun all day dreaming. Of what, I wonder?"

"Hardly the *Medaille d'Or*," I said, remembering that my father's trip to Paris had been to lobby support for his latest bid to capture the prize. He began to go red at the

74

junction of his chin and his collar. His rage rose like water in a basin when you put your foot right down into it. He held in his anger in a rather uncharacteristic display of reserve, and instead turned his sights on another front.

"I hope you enjoyed Avignon, Christian?"

"Yes. I did."

"Good. It's no harm for you to have travelled as far as that this early in your life. From now on, though, there will be no more trips anywhere except Paris at the end of the month until you've begun to earn your keep around here."

I looked at my mother. She looked away and I realised, in that instant, that they had argued about her having allowed me to go. I suspected that whatever meagre portion of affection he had left to give her would be withheld until he satisfied himself of her support in the battle to keep me at Montmirail after my schooling finished. I knew that she'd sworn allegiance to him years ago, but I suppose every now and then I hoped she might reconsider the wisdom of that blind faith. I guessed that her sanctioning of the trip to Avignon marked the very end of her thin supply of independence. When I heard George pottering around outside in the yard, I excused myself from the table and went to join him.

"There's a wild boar in the wood behind my house," he said, as I approached. He held a rifle in his hands. He was cleaning the barrel, and the grey-white dirt on the cloth sparkled as it fell to the ground.

"There's a wild boar in Montmirail too," I said. "If you're quick, you'll get a clean shot at him as he grazes unsuspectingly on his cheese."

"You're funny, Christian. I know you're not serious about these things, but you make great jokes." He clapped me on the back with one of his huge hands.

"Want to come and help me kill it?" he asked.

"Only if you return the favour."

We left the courtyard and went through the arch to the edge of the estate and set our sights on wild meat. The gun

75

made me think of Eugene, and somehow George sensed my thoughts.

"You miss him, don't you?"

"Very much, George. I just wish he were here or that he'd never gone to war. Sometimes I even wish I'd gone in his place. Maybe I'd have survived."

"I'm sure you would," George said, gently. "I'm sure you would."

I wondered whether Eugene had killed anyone during the war. Had he wandered that landscape of death, patrolling for some victim to come along? Had he marched with his comrades and tried to dislodge the Germans from some hill or plateau? Had he inflicted some damage himself before his own life ended? I found it hard to imagine his lining someone up and pulling the trigger. Even harder still was to countenance the idea that he'd taken a life at close quarters: bayonet to heart, revolver to face, hands to throat. Why couldn't I just be satisfied in thinking that he'd walked shoulder to shoulder with other heroes and fallen? What is it about death that demands explanation? What mystifies or terrifies us so that the minute details are required to bring closure? Perhaps that's just it; we need to know everything about the moment of death because we really know so little about death itself, or what lies beyond it.

I READ out my project to my schoolmates in the next-to-last geography class of my life. I tried to avoid her eyes, but couldn't. Even the casual timbre of her voice swept me back to Avignon.

"Thank you, Christian. I'm glad you won the prize and I hope you enjoyed the trip."

"Yes, Miss," I replied. "It was great."

My fear that someone in the school would find out had been revived a couple of days earlier. Ferrier had leaned over to me when I was having a pee in the school toilets.

"Hey, Aragon. Did you give her the treatment when you were in Avignon?"

"Did I give what to who in Avignon?"

"Miss Ore-Production-in-the-Ruhr, who do you think? The teacher and the pupil, you know?"

"Oh, yes, I forgot," I said. "We ate chocolates off each other's naked bodies, and finally made it in a confessional box in a chapel on the Pont St. Bénézet."

"Rubbish," he leered. "I knew nothing would happen; you're not her type, you're too ugly."

I was glad of the dismissive view of Charles Ferrier. I was worried, however, about the priest. He'd certainly seen us, although he might not have been sure who we were, as the train was still moving at the time. It was a thin hope. I encountered him in the corridor of the school on the day I'd presented my project to the class.

"Ah, young Aragon. I've been meaning to talk to you. Do you have a moment?"

"Not right now, Father, I've got some preparatory work to finish for math. See you later, perhaps?" I didn't mean a word of it, and I somehow felt that if I could just avoid him until the end of the term I'd be fine. But it was not meant to be.

"Christian, isn't it?" The voice surprised me as I drank lemonade on the terrace outside the hotel, delaying my return home after school on the same day. I looked up. The wide brim of the priest's hat hid the sun from most of my face, but I shielded my eyes anyway and pretended to be surprised to see him.

"Yes, Father. It is Christian."

"Good," he said, as he sat down in a chair opposite me across the table. "I suppose you know what I want to discuss with you?" He smiled in a mock benign way.

"Actually, Father, I don't. It's all a mystery to me," I said, in as cool a tone as I could muster. I sipped more than I'd intended from my cold glass.

"Is it a mystery, Christian? You really don't know what I wish to discuss with you?"

I didn't reply further.

"Let me help you then," he said. "Because, make no mistake about it, Christian. You do need help. You need protection and guidance and advice. You are the real victim here. She is the instrument of evil."

"I don't know what—"

He stopped me by slamming his open hand on the table between us. "Please, don't compound this situation by lying. I need to know everything so that I can help you. When were you last at confession?"

I could feel the laughter beginning right down in my toes. It crept up through the veins in my legs until it lodged in my throat and tried to force itself out over my tongue. I managed to turn it into a cough. I almost wanted to tell him the details he sought, but I knew that to do so would have very serious consequences for Vivienne.

"There's nothing to laugh about. This is most serious and I intend to get to the root of it one way or another. You are a white flower in a meadow, and she is a sow who has defiled you and taken advantage of your soul. And your body."

He leaned in at me over the table. There was the faint smell of alcohol from him, as he began to whisper in a hoarse, strangled voice which frightened me a little. "If you think that nobody will find out what is going on, then you are very much mistaken. I will make it my primary concern to find out. Your mortal soul is in peril. I cannot tell you how much God wants to bathe you in salvation, but even now your foolish decision to engage in wrong and dishonest acts is driving you further from Him. I cannot allow it. I will not allow it. Do you wish me to speak to your parents about this?"

"Do what you like, Father. Speak to whoever you wish, but I have to repeat that I do not know what you are talking about. I really most sincerely do not."

To be honest, I was frightened more by his demeanour as he spoke than by what he said. I knew that if he approached my parents and made these allegations, my father might just as easily lose his temper and beat the priest to a pulp, as believe every word and seek me out to punish me. The priest's eyes were set deeply into his face, as though straggling behind his other features in hesitation or fatigue. Even taking into account the sight of us kissing on the platform at Avignon, he was still not on firm ground with his accusation. If he'd been standing right beside us and had photographed the moment, he couldn't know anything more than that, unless someone told him.

The only people who could betray us now were ourselves. I sensed too that each denial by me or any expression of ignorance as to what he was talking about, forced him backwards a couple of steps. What did concern me were his tone, his malice, and his clear determination to act on his suspicions. Perhaps the sexual rebellion in the classroom was now driving him to take revenge where he saw weakness, in the ranks of the adolescents who had mocked and frustrated him.

I did not know for sure, but I was worried. Vivienne was the other key to his suspicions and I realised that we would have to meet, sooner rather than later, to plan a united defence to his threats. I was not concerned so much as to what might happen to me, but I feared the impact the priest's accusations would have on Vivienne if the truth were revealed. I knew that I loved her, there was no doubt about that, but I began to feel afraid that I would lose her. Two nights of lovemaking in Avignon may not seem like much to others towards forging an enduring relationship, but for me it was the physical realisation of a previously inchoate love.

We had discussed the priest on the train trip back to Orange, but came to the conclusion that he could not have been sure about what he'd seen given the crowds on the platform and the motion of the train. Father Leterrier's entreaty to me to confess my liaison to him led me to the conclusion that if we told him nothing then he could do nothing and find out no more than he already knew. What would the consequences be for Vivienne if it were known publicly that she'd become involved with one of her pupils? I could only guess that she would lose her job at the school. I wondered if that bastard of a priest might be curious enough to make enquiries at the Hôtel St. Sauveur. I knew too that he had influence at the school and would probably be able to persuade the Board of Governors to get rid of her if he wanted. At least Herve Duchen would have to support the position we had adopted if he were questioned. In my opinion, it was nobody else's business who I fell in love with or who Vivienne chose to allow to eat pralines from her nipples.

"This is our last class together."

Miss Pleyben spoke in a slow matter-of-fact tone. The rest of the class seemed bored, but I was not. I watched as she walked over and back between the blackboard and the table, pointing at maps and making notes on the board about the upgrading of canal connections near Bordeaux. Each movement of her hips reminded me of our lovemaking and I longed to stand up and say, 'Myself and Miss Pleyben are getting married and you're all invited.' Imagine what would have happened. The girls would have begun to cry perhaps and the boys might have applauded. I don't know. In any event, I said nothing.

As the bell rang and the class came to an end, I glanced up at her and tried to make eye contact. She avoided my eyes and handed out our end-of-year cards which contained the seat numbers for the exams the following week. As I took mine from her, I noted a look in her eyes which seemed to direct me to linger. I went out and then came back, past Elise Morel, who was the last to leave the room. Vivienne was gathering her books from the table and the last chunk of chalk lay on the edge, like a mouse about to jump. I went to the back of the room and searched fruitlessly for a pencil I had not lost. When I prepared to leave the room I saw Vivienne at the blackboard, writing. She wrote, 'Lime, Saturday, 3,' and wiped it away when she saw I'd seen it. We had not discussed how we might communicate, but this at least was clear. I knew that in a few days I'd no longer be a schoolboy, and I couldn't wait to be alone and lie with her again.

"The *Concours National* is only five days away, now," my mother said that evening at supper. My father lifted his head. He was dipping bread in a bowl of olive oil and he looked diagonally across the table at me.

"You're coming to Paris, Christian, I assume?"

"No, Papa. I have an exam on the twenty-sixth, so I'll have to stay in Gigondas." I didn't look up as I spoke.

"Exams! What bloody use are they to you? You don't need—"

My mother made a rare intervention. "Robert. I thought we agreed that Christian would finish all of the exams."

My father snorted and then smirked. "Alright. That's fine. But the very next day you'll be working on the estate. When I return from Paris on the twenty-eighth, you and I will sit down with George and come up with a plan to take us through the next year. It's about time you started to accept responsibility, Boy. This work is hard and physical, but if you're going to own Montmirail someday, then your investment of time and work cannot begin soon enough."

"And if I don't want to own Montmirail some day?" I asked, in a soft voice.

My father's sweeping arm knocked over a bottle of wine and the bowl of oil as he rose and pushed back his chair, and stood to dominate the room and his family. The wine rushed to the edge of the table and began to drip onto the floor like thin blood. The oil seemed content to restrict itself to the tabletop.

"I have worked for thirty-five years with this red soil and heavy sun. I have sweated so that you and your mother can have food, a roof, comfort. Don't you dare defy me in this now, Christian. Your brother would have done anything to be alive today and working in those fields. He understood that family, loyalty, inheritance, pride and blood are what we are all about. He died so that runts like you could live in a free country. You will take your place in this family, even if I have to beat these values and this obligation into you. Do you hear me?"

I didn't reply. I rose from the table, and walked out of the room to the salon at the front of the house where the good china cups were kept in a cupboard. The empty fireplace lay cold in the summer, near the good chairs and the small shelf of books nobody read. My temper was provoked, but I knew that I could not do anything yet. I felt the heat of his words on my face and I saw my scar in the mirror near the door. I sat down on the expensive seat by the window, and looked out at the front garden of Montmirail to where the sunshine had driven a cat to nap under a stone trough for shade. I wanted to close my eyes and fly away, but knew that I couldn't. The battle was coming closer now, and very soon I would have to fight or run. I needed Vivienne, and I needed to speak with her right away.

My mind was a muddle. My head pounded with my father's words echoing inside it, 'Loyalty, inheritance, pride.' What was that all about? How could I feel loyalty to a world bordered only by obligation and fear? I wasn't a willing participant in any of this. I wanted to do something else, to travel, to love, to be free. Okay, so I had no great plan ahead of me, but within that void lay the possibilities of my own life choices and errors. Even that vague future was preferable to having inheritance cast upon me like a yoke. What about Vivienne? Surely she had the right to determine her own destiny and to choose who to be with? I could not begin to imagine what would happen in my family if I simply declared my love for her, and refused to be a part of Montmirail and its duties.

What became increasingly clear to me now was that we would have to leave Gigondas if we were to have a life together. The priest and the rest of the village, or my father's wrath and my mother's indifference, could not provide a sound basis for our future here. They guaranteed its failure. I knew that I would have to go elsewhere and start a life on my own. If I stayed, I would crumble like the soil in the sun, and eventually be trampled into becoming part of the cycle—whether I liked it or not. I would be cut back in April and harvested in September, year-in, year-out, while my father stood watch over me, waiting until I succumbed enough to the past to be trusted with the future.

Could I be a doctor, as George had suggested, or a soldier like Eugene? Any bloody thing was possible as long as I made the choice myself. I was nearly my own person now, and a couple of exams and hard days and nights alone stood between me and forever. I knew that Vivienne and I could be together and that if we were, then I would be happy. Even picking stones out of the gardens of rich widows in Marseille would be better than the comfort offered by remaining here and engaging with the fantasy of gold medals each July!

The lime tree lay on the right-hand side of the rough path that cut up into the Dentelles above the village. The needle-like points of the mountains arched like so many spires over the top of the pine forest below, and reached up into the Saturday afternoon sky. I was there almost an hour before the appointed time, and sat out of view from the path on a slope that led up into the pines. Huddled there in the shade the absolute silence cocooned me from the universe.

The uneven scraping of wooden wheels on stones roused me from my trance. Monsieur Alombert lived alone in the village and collected firewood from the forests and sold it door-to-door. Most people could have collected it themselves for free, but gave him a couple of francs to keep him alive. He walked ahead of the cart. The tired mule between the shafts of the vehicle followed him at a pace that suited both of them because of their age. I watched them disappear over the crest of the hill and as soon as they vanished from view, Vivienne came walking up slowly towards the lime tree. I whistled softly and she stepped off the track and looked over her shoulder cautiously, before ascending the slope to join me. I had been afraid that she mightn't love me any longer because of the time we'd been apart. I need not have worried. We kissed before we spoke, and an urgency held us both as we lowered ourselves to the ground and embraced as tightly as I could ever remember us having done.

"Vivienne," I began. "I've missed you so much. I need to talk to you about Fr. Leterrier."

She silenced me with a kiss and then took my hand. "It's dangerous here," she said. "Someone might hear us, we've got to go up into the forest. No one must see us."

We stood, and she brushed some pine needles from my shirt and held both of my hands, and looked at me the way a mother might. We walked over the dry undergrowth with the cracking of twigs and the rustle of dry grass an accompaniment to our thoughts. When we were deep among the trees, we found a clearing and sat side by side, and spoke of the future and the present and the fear surrounding both.

"Fr. Leterrier has been to see me, Christian. He knows about us, or at least thinks he knows. He's spoken to Duchen. Herve told him that he was with us and that nothing happened, but Leterrier is still unshaken in his suspicions. Of course, Herve is curious now too. The priest says that he will go to the school authorities and have me dismissed. He says he can prevent my ever working as a teacher again in France. He's obsessed with us. He says I've stolen your soul. He wants me to leave Gigondas."

"I know. He's spoken to me too."

"Where? When? What did you tell him?"

"Nothing." I laughed. "Not even when he asked me when I'd last made my confession."

"Christian, this is serious." Her eyes widened in alarm. "If they . . . if the school authorities find out, I'll lose my job and I'll never teach anywhere again. The school is rented from the priests so they have an enormous power. We must be careful. I'm sorry now that I—"

"Sorry that you and I?"

"No." She shook her head. "I'm not sorry about any of that. But I'm afraid that if the priest pursues this, he may involve the police, the school, and the education ministry." She wiped a single tear from her cheek with the back of her hand. "You're only a boy, not yet seventeen. I'm your teacher and I'm responsible for—"

"My mortal soul?"

"Yes. Yes. I suppose so," she said. "It's such a mess, all of this now."

I told her about Fr. Leterrier's outburst outside the hotel. I told her how I'd made a decision to leave the village if I had to, in order to be free—in order to be with her.

"And what will we live on? Fresh-Air Pie?"

"You can teach and I'll find some kind of work. I'll even pick stones from the gardens of rich widows in Marseille if I have to. We'll be fine and we'll be together."

"And what about your family? Your inheritance?"

"My inheritance?" I laughed. "My *family* is my inheritance, and I want no part of it now. I don't care if I never see them again. It's not them I want. I want you. I love you, Vivienne."

She stopped talking and she stared at me. Then she leaned in to whisper into my ear, although no one but me would have heard her even if she'd shouted. "And I love you too, Christian. I love you."

She began to unbutton her blouse, and under the shade of two huge pine trees I laid out the blanket I'd taken from the airing cupboard. The sunlight infiltrated the cones on the branches and eased its way deep into the forest, where it spread its warmth around us like an angel.

CHAPTER EIGHT

If someone crept up on me in the middle of the night and nailed my hands to the bedposts and told me not to see her again, I would gnaw my hands off at the elbow and run to her with my limbs trailing blood through this tiny village. I might have been a bird down at the sea or up over the Dentelles, or a boy who was able to fly: I flew like mad up, up, up over the village, and swooped down and landed on a window ledge and saw myself through the glass huddled over a math paper I did not understand. Eugene was in some faraway place, as were the millions and millions of other souls who had absconded in death at the Somme or the Marne or Verdun. There was a famous recruitment poster designed by Faivre and it was everywhere during the war. The picture showed a man in civilian headdress with an army greatcoat and a rifle, rushing forward and urging France to follow with the slogan, WE HAVE THEM. I remembered thinking, at one time, that he was beckoning the dead to follow and giving them heart with the cry of WE HAVE THEM, meaning something dead people needed, like blocks of ice in hell or white shirts to wear in heaven. I saw Eugene's face in the math paper where the numbers gathered in the centre of the page and rearranged themselves into his features. My lover was beneath me on a bed of pinecones and math papers. I was aching to see her again.

"Five minutes," Herve Duchen said, signalling the final moments of my education. I wondered what position his mistress on the Boulevard St. Jacques liked best when he was hard and ready for her. Perhaps she preferred it from behind and waited on all fours for him on silk sheets in a rented room, until he announced his arrival and the anticipated duration of the act: 'Five minutes.' I was angry with the world and he was an easy target. I remembered that he had helped us thwart the priest, and I regretted my anger that came from a different source entirely.

My father had tried to re-establish the ground rules for the future when he came unannounced into my bedroom on the previous morning.

"We're going to Paris."

"I know," I replied. I struggled to adjust my eyes against the light as he opened the shutters on the window.

"When I return, I expect to see the four hectares above the church cleared of rabbits. George will show you what to do when that's finished."

"I—"

"Please don't waste your breath, Christian. I'm tired of your stories and excuses. I've waited long enough for you to finish at that damned school. You will now do the things your brother would have undertaken gladly. That's the end of it."

"I'm not Eugene," I shouted as he turned and left the room.

He hesitated, and then glanced back bitterly over his shoulder. "That has been all too apparent for a considerable time, Christian. But, I'm afraid Montmirail will just have to make the best of it. There's no alternative."

I wanted to run after him and beat him on the face with my fists, and shout into his ears about how I missed my brother too, and how this mess was not of my making. But I did not do that. I was beginning to make my own plans about cutting this place from my life like a petrified twig pruned from the vine between December and March. I was not destined to crush grapes.

After the math exam, we exited into the voracious sunshine. The noon heat cradled the class as a unit for the last time on the front steps of our lycée. Some students began to shake hands and embrace, marking the moment with a sort of uncertain affection. I felt my hand pressed and my cheek kissed, but I could not tell you now, nor could I have identified then, who the kissers or the shakers were.

Couderc's mother was standing outside the gates of the school as I left. Her son should have been graduating with us, but his lungs had exercised first refusal on his life. She stared at me. I nodded and instinctively reached for my scar with a finger.

"You can hardly see it now, Christian." She smiled and spoke as I touched my cheek. I was unsure as to the appropriate response, so I moved my finger to my forehead and flicked my hair back like I wasn't even looking for the scar. In her eyes I saw the loss of her son. Without warning, she was enveloped by a cascade of children who rushed by with skipping ropes and hoops.

Down in the village, the mayor was dressed in his full ceremonial robes. He had invited the parents of the graduating class to drink wine at the *Mairie* while their offspring tackled mathematics. Elise Morel's mother was a big lady with cheeks as red as roof tiles. She walked up and down the village square looking anxiously in the direction of the school for a sign of her daughter. I could make out some of the other parents, but I knew my mother would not have been there even if she hadn't gone to Paris to attend the annual embarrassment of the *Concours National*.

Twenty minutes later, I had doubled back behind the hotel and made my way past Domaine de la Mavette to the Vacqueyras Road. My shoes hurt and I took them off and walked barefoot on the warm dust. The Chapel of St. Cosme was like a permanent sentinel at the edge of my world. I eyed it with relief; it grew in size as I neared, and I recalled how small I'd felt beside it when I was a child. My temperature soared, and my heart stalled and restarted as I contemplated my future. My head pounded and echoed my footfall in tempo as something beyond my control caused my decision and my feelings about it to oscillate over and back in a small space directly in front of my eyes. I wanted to run and hide, and then to stay and confront, and all at once I was gripped by a palpable sense of despair as I wondered what damage I would cause in her life because of my love for her. She was older, yes. But perhaps I was stronger than I imagined, bolder than I deserved to be. Was I a hunter-gatherer, stalking, following, watching, kissing, coveting, loving her? Or was it part of some grand design that God hatched for me—to compensate me for the loss of my brother? Could it be that I was powerless to resist or to vary the course? Was I the driving force behind this pattern of action we'd embarked upon? Perhaps it was my fault rather than our fortune or destiny. The thing we share: do we create it, or is it already there and waiting to be eaten?

I would justify my decision to my father. I would challenge his myopia and lay my own desires before him. I couldn't run away like a child or a coward. No, I'd have to be open and honest about it, and choose my life in the confident glare of the sun—not pilfer it in the cowardly hue of darkness.

"Father, I have something to say." I rehearsed out loud as I climbed the incline to the rear of the church. "I am in love with someone and I want to be with her. I cannot be who you imagine me to be. I am nearly seventeen, and I will not be moulded by you to chaperone these eleven hectares into a harvest of my own blood."

"That sounded good."

I started. Vivienne was in the archway of the sacristy door. She'd clearly enjoyed my monologue. Her smile lit up the alcove and she stepped forward to take my hand. We kissed.

"How was math?" she asked.

"I was rehearsing what I'd say to my father when he returns from Paris," I said, answering a question she'd never asked.

"Christian, are you sure you want to go through with this?"

"More sure than ever," I replied.

The chapel was locked, as it often was during the week. This stone house of worship leaned out over the village into the day like a nosy neighbour. I used my knife to lift the latch on the shutters of the sacristy, and as it flipped back with a tiny noise, the wind suddenly blew up and caught the inside of the shutters. They opened out towards me and knocked me off balance. I almost fell to the ground. The noise of the shutters slamming in the wind seemed to me to be loud enough to echo across the village, or at least down onto the Vacqueyras Road. But I need not have concerned myself. The rest of the world was somewhere else and we had the place to ourselves.

Inside, the chapel was cold but it was not damp or musty. The air was chilled and refreshing. The empty pews awaited us as we opened the door fully from the anteroom to the altar. A pair of brass candelabras stood on the marble table of worship, and further down the church, over the baptismal font, the room edged upwards and out at the sky through two narrow windows above the main door. I remembered Avignon. Vivienne touched her lips with a finger and hushed me to listen to the sounds of the moment. A bird twittered in the rafters and the Mistral insinuated itself into the little chapel and surrounded us in a swish. Tiny details of the place remain with me in lighted prominence, protruding out of the scene like embossed letters on expensive paper. I recall a purple sash draped over a velvet-upholstered chair where a priest might have sat. On the warm mosaic tiles that depicted the biblical scene of the flight from Egypt, my bare, dusty feet left tracks. A drizzle of dust danced in a sliver of sunshine and sparkled to its death on the floor of the aisle. We sat on the edge of the raised level of the altar and held hands and talked. Fr. Leterrier had confronted her again.

"I saw something in his expression this time which frightened me," Vivienne said.

"Maybe the same thing I saw on the terrace at the hotel."

"Something I can't quite describe worried me about his voice and his threats this time, Christian. I thought that he would grow weaker in his accusations and that I would—"

"Prosper in your defence?" I offered.

"Exactly. But it was as if he had gained the actual knowledge by my denial or rebuke. I can't explain it but—"

"There's no need, Vivienne. It's like me and my imaginary conversations with my father. It's only a rehearsal, not real, until I stand toe to toe with him and face him down with my dream, my choice, my—"

"Life?"

"Yes. Yes," I said, with a nervous laugh. "That's it. I'm just marking time until I tell him who I am and what I am going to do."

"And what you've done?" She smiled.

I thought about it for a moment. "Well, maybe not everything. Not yet. It would be too much for him." I smiled inwardly, thinking of how my father might react if I told him all of the details of our trip to Avignon. In time, perhaps very soon, he would come to imagine and reckon these things for himself. To be honest, I simply wanted to discharge my bare duty as a son and tell him I was leaving and why. After that, his impressions or suspicions or concerns were entirely a matter for himself.

"I'm going to leave the school," she said.

I watched her lips release the words, and anticipated that they would leave a fine trace of regret or uncertainty behind on her mouth. I saw none. "Are you sure?"

"Yes. I've thought about it, and I see now that we must leave Gigondas if we're to have any real chance of happiness."

"And what about your house?"

"Monsieur Vaton has often asked me to sell it to him. I'm sure he would revive his offer at a moment's notice. The Notaire will transfer it into my name to allow a sale."

At that exact moment, an uncertainty had bumped off my soul and receded a little. But still it spun like a top at the edge of my line of sight, and threatened to return. I was strong one minute and crippled the next, vacillating between love and desire on the one hand, and fear on the other. I was out now in the thick of my own life, and this passionate beautiful woman, seven years my senior, was throwing away her life this far in order to begin again with me. As the bride abandons her father's arm at the door of the church, the symbolism of that leap from past to future was now all about us. Here, in a tiny church overlooking a tiny village at the foot of a mountain range, I was about to jump into my future with the comfort of this woman, and the discomfort of the damage I might do to her life by joining it with mine.

Montmirail was just a house, and to be frank, all that lived in it was the dust of a family disintegrated long ago. Eugene had been the soul of that place. It was he and no one else who had brought Christmas alive there, and made the harvesting of the grapes seem worthwhile and good. He had supplied life from his own store of it. The war and the rain, and the trenched damp that plucked him out of our lives had not been of his making. His death had not been his own choice, and his absence from our lives now was no one's fault. He had lived as long as he could and that was all there was to it. I slept in his bedroom and perhaps he slept there still, and infused my sleep with a dead corporal's strength. It was not my house, anyway. I knew that. The rooms were a committee of spaces and divisions; the entire was only the sum of the parts, and the plaster barriers and creaking presence of stairs and doors, only hummed along with each other. For me, they provided no sense of belonging anymore. The trees in the avenue and the sunshine through the dining room windows were all I counted as precious in Montmirail. What happiness I'd had there was a distant memory, and the calculated and vitriolic silence of my parents' union was not a thing I cared to live beneath for a moment longer than necessary. If I continued to live with my father, it would only be a matter of time before he battered me into the type of son he really wanted. Only George drew me to the place now, with his big hands and enormous heart. I would miss him and maybe he would miss me, but he had settled a life for himself there, and to be fair, it did not depend on me in any way for its survival.

Vivienne and I held hands and stood up on the step below the altar. She took a ring for me from one of the tiny pockets of her dress. I had made one for her from one of the hinges of the chest in which we kept Eugene's things. The hinge was broken and made from light metal. I'd hammered it and heated it, then wrapped it around a piece of cork and fired it in embers before cooling it in water. I hoped it would fit her. It may sound like a clumsy token, but it was all that I could think to do, besides stealing from my mother; and that would have been an awful lapse of independence.

We placed the rings on each other's fingers and promised to take each other and hold the promise in our hearts; to worship each other with our bodies and our minds, until the unwelcome shadow of death cut us off from the sun. It was a simple exchange—made hundreds of years after Pierre of Provence and Princess Maguelone had done the same on the site where Montmirail now stood. I had thought of trying to replicate the exchange, in the kitchen or even the bedroom of the house in my parents' absence, but I decided against it. I felt it might in some tacit way represent an honouring of the house by me, and I did not want that. Also, I felt that it would require revisiting the house at some future time, and I did not intend coming back. The Chapel of St. Cosme was quiet, private—and above all—symbolised for me the making of a commitment before God. We would someday, I hoped, be married in a proper ceremony by a priest who neither knew us nor disapproved of our union. Every place, from a hamlet to Paris had a church, so that no matter where we ended up, there would be a place to go when we needed a touchstone or a renewal of our vows.

"So I'm Madame Aragon now. Am I?"

"Oh, no. I didn't think of that. Perhaps I'll be Monsieur Pleyben, instead."

We stood silently for a short time regarding each other in an altogether different way. I thought about the essential ingredient for a valid marriage. So did she.

"I'd like you to come and spend the night at my house. Our house." She invited me with a trace of nervousness I had not detected before. It would be the perfect way to say goodbye to the place where she had lived.

It was agreed. I would return to the village and make an appearance at the festivities before going to Montmirail to pack a small bag. We would leave in a day or two, after my parents returned and I had delivered the news to my father. I couldn't run away or elope. That would be cowardly and easy, and ultimately, I suspected it would destroy me from the inside out. Facing my father would be the most difficult thing I'd ever chosen to do, but it had to be done to complete the circle of the decision-making process. I would say goodbye to George. Perhaps I would even help him clear the rabbits as the last act the pair of us would do together of the work I was choosing to abandon. He deserved the courtesy of an explanation, and I could easily imagine maintaining a correspondence with him in the future. How else would I learn of my parents' deaths?

We left the church and returned to the village separately. I thought about the sacrifice she was making in leaving her position at the school. She would surely find another job somewhere. She was a marvellous teacher. I wondered what would happen if my father tried to physically stop me from leaving Gigondas with her. Surely he would not be able to restrain me? Would he even try? I tried not to think too much about it. I would deal with it when it happened, if it happened.

The festivities were in full swing. A man from Seguret with an accordion played polkas and the villagers danced.

I eased through the crowd and smiled and nodded without saying a word. Strong fingers gripped my arm.

"Eh, Aragon. Why aren't you drinking?" Ferrier held onto me, waiting for a reply. When I said nothing, he simply pushed me aside and returned to the long table at the edge of the gathering where the wine was being poured and spilled.

I saw Elise Morel and her mother dancing together. Abel Beaumet was swinging a tiny girl in a display of dancing that was comical, but also tinged with a sexual energy. It was a force I doubted would have possessed him without the mix of graduation and alcohol. The mayor had abandoned his ceremonial robes and I think I saw his wife somewhere else, just watching him enjoying himself. It was close to the spot from where I'd observed the fizz rockets and Catherine wheels explode above us on the night when Vivienne had stood beside me on the Saints' day.

This was my goodbye, my passage from graduation to adulthood. I took in the sight of the people, I drank it up like a memory to be stored for later when I needed to remember where I'd come from, and who I was or might have been. I turned from the crowd and ambled into the Place de la Fontaine. I'd gone to Montmirail first and packed a bag and left it beside the fountain. I splashed my face with water from the fountain, and leaned backwards over the stone basin to drink from the cold water that trickled out of the mouth of a small lion.

When I could drink no more, I picked up my bag and made my way past the graveyard and the fever hospice to the track which led to the mountains. I looked over the wall of the cemetery and tried to find Couderc's headstone. Instead, the first grave I rested my eyes upon was Eugene's. I never came to see him there. I always spoke with him like he was a ghost or a cloud or something like smoke, all around, but moving and still alive in some curious comforting way. The headstone and the plot were too cold for me. They called it his resting place, but he wasn't even in the grave. His uniform, lying there crumpled in a box in the ground, was not him. In fact, it was almost a perfect acknowledgement of his absence. He was somewhere else, so I could not even begin to imagine him here in the cemetery. I think I would have found it almost impossible to leave Gigondas if he really had been buried there.

The track grew steep and I saw the Dentelles in their white splendour. About halfway from the village to Vivienne's small house, I stopped and took a pee in the bushes. As I emerged out onto the track, a figure came down the hill towards me. It was the priest. We kept walking until we were face-to-face and I saw a cruel smile begin to invade his features.

"Ah, Mr. Aragon. Isn't it?"

"Yes?"

I saw him look at my bag held at my side like a piece of game. I knew now that he knew all about us. If I'd ever doubted it. Vivienne had been correct.

"Off on holidays, I suppose?" he said with a sneer. I said nothing. He nodded back in the direction of the house. "You'll be going alone. I think she's changed her mind."

I immediately thought that he'd injured her.

"Priest, if you've harmed her, I'll kill you," I said calmly. I began to run up the hill in my bare feet as he continued on his way. What the hell has he been doing visiting her, I wondered. I was short of breath when I reached the house and I went around to the rear. I could hear raised voices, but the words were indistinct. I pushed the door open. Vivienne was cowering in the corner of the kitchen. A man stood over her with a pine branch in his hand.

"Don't touch her," I warned. He turned around. It was her husband, Stephane. He smiled through his rage.

"So, it's the little bastard who's been fucking my wife, is it?"

He advanced in my direction and threw the branch to the ground. He reached into his belt where I saw a knife in a sheath.

"Run, Christian, run!" Vivienne screamed.

He turned back to her and kicked out at her face with his boot. I could not see if he made contact, but I did see that her forearm was already bleeding. I reached into my pocket and found my own knife. In a flash it was open. I charged forward at him and knocked him into the wall where he stumbled and lost his balance. When he got to his feet, I saw that the knife from his belt was in his hand. He was taller than me and a good bit heavier. I weighed up my chances. His was a hunting knife and had a polished wooden handle. I remember thinking for a second about throwing mine at him and hoping for the best. But we were too close. There was a small saucepan on the table and it looked to be full of liquid. I tried to put my free hand out to grab it as we circled each other like prizefighters, both unsure of what to do next.

"You thought you'd move into my house, did you?" he snarled as he looked down at my bag.

I swung the pan up and across the table and into his face, and tried to push the table at him as well. But it collapsed. Suddenly, we were at each other on the broken table—grappling, struggling, kicking, biting and roaring like wild animals. There was a clatter as he lost his knife, and I remember his face in mine. I became conscious of the smell of soup coming up at us from the floor where the saucepan had overturned. I head-butted him, hoping to break his nose and he fell backwards. The last movement of the oak table beneath us favoured me, and I finished falling by rolling across him. He landed heavily, striking his head, and as he collapsed his eyes spoke of the horror to come if he lived. My knife was at his throat. Seconds later, he was between two worlds, blood spurting up at me out of his neck. He was dead in a matter of moments, lying on the floor of the house he'd fled from to avoid conscription in the Great War.

CHAPTER NINE

The trial was held in August 1921, in the Palais de Justice in Carpentras in the Cour d'Assises. It was the same courtroom where five soldiers from Eugene's battalion had been tried for desertion and treason two weeks after the war had ended. My father had gone to Carpentras for that trial, and had bathed in the horror of their execution less than twenty minutes after the verdict had been brought in. They had been lined up against the rear wall of the Cathédrale St. Siffrein. For my father it was an opportunity to revel in the memory of his heroic son, as he watched France sacrifice cowards in order to honour the brave.

From the date of my arrest in July of the previous year, until the beginning of the trial on August eleventh, I had been held in the fourteenth-century prison on the Rue du Château. My cell was small and damp, and the barred window some eight feet above the floor gave a singular if unappealing view of the Porte d'Orange. I would dearly like, in dramatic terms, to infuse my account now with tales of wild mistreatment and the daily challenge of battles with rats and disease, but I cannot, because that is not how it was. The fact that I was awaiting trial and not serving a sentence upon conviction meant that I was a guest of the prison, in the legal sense at least. I was housed in the most benign of its accommodations. The aroma of the plane and lotus trees from the Place d'Inguimbert delighted me for both summers, and on countless evenings during all of my incarceration awaiting trial, somebody—a child, perhaps—threw black olives at my window with varying degrees of accuracy. My eyes were, in one way, my greatest hindrance. When they were open I saw only stone and straw. When they were closed, however, I was transported back to the pine forest at the foot of the Dentelles where we'd made love, or to the gushing water from the fountain on the little street off the main square in Gigondas.

Vivienne was a constant source of calm and reassurance, and her monthly visits punctuated my stay. Each time she came to the prison we were closely supervised by warders. We made every effort to convey our feelings across the cold stone table, where intimacy was impossible. On her final visit before the trial we talked for the first time about what it would be like.

"Are you afraid, Christian?"

"Not really. A little though, I suppose." She took my hands across the table, and although one warder seemed about to rebuke us and make us disengage, a look from the other seemed to satisfy him that there was no security threat posed by the contact.

"Don't worry, Christian. Everything will work out."

"I know. I know."

"What does Monsieur Jourdic say?" Leopold Jourdic was my lawyer.

"He's hopeful, but it's hard to read him, you know. He talks a lot, but doesn't really say much that I can hold onto."

Jourdic was the public defender for the Vaucluse region. My family was not going to pay for a lawyer from Paris or Marseille, so the defence of my case was in his hands, and paid for by the taxes of everybody in the region. I think that even had my family offered to pay for my defence, I would have refused their help. It would have been a renunciation of the choices I had made for myself if I sought or accepted their assistance now. Anyway, the predicament in which I found myself was pretty much all of my own making.

Monsieur Jourdic was originally from the Ardèche. He had a reputation for being a hard-nosed lawyer who never gave up on any of his clients until they were acquitted, or *La*

Veuve—the widow—had cut off their heads. Neither Vivienne nor myself knew anything about the law, and so we placed our complete trust in Leopold Jourdic and hoped for the best. My pre-trial consultations with him had been long and to the point in a roundabout way. He lectured me on the law, the guillotine, and sometimes recounted stories of past triumphs, and it should be said, some failures, too.

"I had one particular client, Henriette Gontier," Jourdic told me in one of our meetings, "who was accused of poisoning her husband with salt. I knew in my soul that she was not guilty; she had no trace of malice, no hint of evil about her. The trial lasted three weeks and the defence hinged on the evidence of an apothecary from Rouen who was supposed to be an expert on salt. He was a disaster in the witness-box. He gave evidence in such an evasive manner that it appeared to the jury he was telling untruths. Later, we learned that he was his own best customer in the supply of opium, but by then it was too late. Henriette lost her life because of the incompetence of someone else. We might even have won if we hadn't called him to the stand at all." He shook his head sadly.

Between anecdotes from his brilliant career, Monsieur Jourdic and I discussed tactics. We debated whether I should give evidence at the trial.

"Much of it depends on the prosecution's case. We may not know until it ends whether or not you should testify, Christian."

"Won't it seem strange to the jury if I don't give evidence?"

"They are not allowed to draw an adverse inference from your refusal. The judges will instruct them on that point."

"But all the same—surely it's to my advantage?"

"The things that are to your advantage in my view are your age, possibly making the claim of self-defence, and your relationship with this lady, the wife of the deceased."

"Vivienne."

"Yes, Madame Pleyben. Now if the jury sees you as the impressionable young schoolboy seduced by this older woman, and then provoked into killing her estranged husband in a fit of anger and—"

"Passion?"

"Yes, that's it, passion, Christian. Passion. This is the emotion at the heart of our being. As Frenchmen, Christian, we are driven to achievement and to anger because of our passion. Our hearts are the charioteers of our destiny."

He looked down momentarily and then up again to gauge my reaction. I could feel him beginning to formulate his closing remarks to the jury. With the addition, perhaps, of some tinkering later on for effect, I felt I'd been treated to the bones of his final submissions to the court.

"No," I said.

"No?"

"No. I won't let her be dragged into this."

"She's *already* in this, Christian. If she gives evidence in your defence, then you may be acquitted. I know that she wasn't in the house when the fight occurred. She was—"

"In the outhouse, and then went to the well near the trees." I finished the sentence for him.

"Yes. I have read her statement, and she would seem to be of no use to the prosecution as a witness. However, she is central to any attempt by us to paint the full picture for the jury."

"Of what use is it to call her when she can say nothing about the fight and the death of her husband?"

"The jury will want to know what passed between her and the deceased after the priest left. The mood of the husband seems to have been very aggressive, but I need the jury to hear it from her own mouth, to listen to her tell of how he said he would 'kill the boy,' as she says in her statement; and how he treated her in the past."

"Vivienne will only be used by the prosecutor to discredit me and to blacken her name. They will try to have the jury believe that she and I planned to kill him—or something like that."

"And did you?"

"Of course not." I was getting angry now.

"Then, why are you afraid of calling her?"

"I don't want her to give evidence because they'll ask her about her relationship with me. She will have to admit certain things and then—"

"If she admits to having sexual relations with one of her underage pupils, then she'll most certainly be prosecuted, yes. But if she does not give evidence on your behalf, then you will probably be convicted of murder and sentenced to death. In any event, she can be called by the prosecution. It is only if you were married that she would not be a compellable witness."

"Perhaps they won't be able to prove the charge," I suggested.

"I wish you were right. But I'm afraid they have substantial evidence against you. I have read the charge, and the prosecutor seems definite about the circumstances. It *was* your knife?"

"Yes."

"And you were holding it when the doctor and the gendarme arrived?"

"Yes."

"You had blood on your clothes and your hands?"

I nodded.

"Then we shall just have to do our best with what we have," he said with a sigh. "See you on Tuesday."

MY ABILITY to fly in my dreams deserted me sometime during the course of that year. I could still imagine myself elsewhere, and dream of being with Vivienne and of making love in the most awkward and strange places: in olive groves, behind barrels of wine at Montmirail, in churches, or the baths at Les Florets. I even saw us once under my parents' bed coupling, while they slept at the extremes of the mattress above. But my own power to fly inside of those dreams, to determine the direction of the dream itself, and to hover above the snippets of life occurring beneath my flight—that vanished. It vanished and I was a prisoner twice.

Apart from Vivienne's visits and the meetings with Monsieur Jourdic, nobody came to see me. My mother wrote to me once to tell me how proud she was of me and how she believed I was innocent. My father wrote to me twice, once to tell me how ashamed he was of me and how he knew I was guilty. The other time he wrote to say how ashamed he was of my mother for having written to me, and how he'd forbidden her to write again. To be honest, I nearly expected her to write a second time expressing her own shame at having written the first time, but that really would have been too much!

"YOU WILL hear, gentlemen, of how this murder was planned down to the last detail. How the accused secured the purchase of the knife weeks earlier in anticipation of the return of Stephane Pleyben. You will learn of the sordid details of the love affair which the accused had with Madame Pleyben. You will also hear about how it drove him to murder her husband, when Monsieur and Madame Pleyben were on the precipice of a reconciliation. All possibility of that reconciliation was ended by a young boy with a knife of steel and a heart of stone."

The prosecutor, Monsieur Icard, was the master of dramatics and overstatement. His track record as a prosecutor of murder charges had the sort of statistics—of success, failure and retrial—that would have worried me as a healthy and fit boxer if he were my opponent. Monsieur Jourdic was a marked contrast in presentation and force, and it seemed to me at least that the case might very well hinge on which of them the jury preferred. The first witness was the doctor.

"I attended at the house of Monsieur and Madame Pleyben at a minute or two past three o'clock in the afternoon. Madame Pleyben had called at my house in quite a state of shock. I was tending to the ingrown toenail of a patient when she arrived. I left immediately, and met Sergeant Bezart just behind the main entrance to the fever hospice. He also was on his way to the house."

"What did you find on arriving there?" Icard looked at the jury when he spoke, giving the impression that he was their instrument, asking the questions they themselves wanted to.

"I found the deceased in a prone position on the floor of the kitchen. He was lying on his back and his left arm was bent around the leg of a heavy table, which was broken, and partially covered his lower body. The leg of the table and the immediate area of the deceased's head and torso were almost entirely covered with blood. From the back of the shoulders, which lay on the floor, for a distance of perhaps two feet outwards, the entire stone paving was splattered with congealed blood in a semi-circular pattern. I examined the body and confirmed that the deceased had died from a single stab wound to the neck. This incision had simultaneously severed a major artery and punctured the windpipe. I concluded that the probable cause of death was a brain hemorrhage from lack of oxygen and partial blood asphyxiation."

"He choked on his own blood?"

"Yes, at least in part. You see—"

"He choked on his own blood. Thank you, Doctor. Now, did you find anyone else at the scene?"

"Yes."

"Who?"

"A young man from the village, Christian Aragon. I know his family for many—"

"The accused. You mean the accused, there?" He pointed at me. The prosecutor was not going to allow me to be described in personal terms. That might humanise me for the jury.

"Yes, the accused. He was sitting on a chair beside the sink area and he had, I don't know if I can say this . . ." The doctor looked to Icard for guidance.

"If you saw something then you *must* say it. If it is true, it must form part of your testimony. You saw the accused. He was sitting on a chair and he had . . . ?"

"A knife. He had a large pocket-knife in his hands." The doctor looked over at me, apologetically. I smiled at him to show I bore him no ill-will.

"Was it the same knife which caused the wound which led to the death of Stephane Pleyben?" The prosecutor paused, and then looked from the jury to the witness and back again, conveying the question and the expectation from the twelve to the doctor.

"Yes. In my opinion it was."

"Did you examine the knife?"

"Not there and then."

"When?"

"Afterwards, in the police station at Carpentras. I was invited by the investigating magistrate," he bowed to the middle judge, "to view the knife and to compare the blade and its dimensions with my notes on the nature and extent of the wound."

"And your conclusion?"

"It was the same knife."

"Thank you, Doctor."

Monsieur Jourdic asked a series of questions about the measurements of the wound, and the work on bloodstains being pioneered in the United States at that time. He was polite and gentle in his cross-examination, and to be honest, he made no real impression of challenging the doctor or his findings. It was almost as if he were simply giving the witness a second opportunity to repeat his quite damning evidence. Including the part about finding me with the knife. All of that was true, of course, and we were not going to challenge the doctor on his account of the truth.

Sergeant Bezart was brief and enthusiastic in the witness box.

"I was invited to the graduation celebration by the mayor, Monsieur de Vay, to supervise the fireworks display later that evening."

"I believe the display was cancelled?"

"Yes."

"Why?" Monsieur Icard feigned ignorance.

"Because of the death of Monsieur Pleyben."

"The *murder* of Monsieur Pleyben. No?"

Jourdic was on his feet in an instant, before the policeman could reply,

"That is a matter for the jury, my lords. Not for this witness, surely?"

The judges nodded and the trial continued. The three judges were all men in late middle age. One of them was silent for the entire trial. The presiding judge was a man of few words, and only spoke when it was absolutely necessary to do so. All evidentiary or procedural disputes were resolved by a conference of nods or shakes of the head. Decisions were made known by the presiding judge pointing his crooked right index finger at the advocate in whose favour they had decided the issue. It was like appearing in front of three mute or very shy ghosts.

"Did the accused say anything to you at the scene?"

"Yes. As I escorted him from the house, and indicated that we would have to meet his parents and inform them of the situation, he said, 'I didn't want to lose her.'"

"He said he didn't want to lose her, is that correct?"

"Yes."

"And who did you understand him to mean?"

"Why, Madame Pleyben, of course."

"Thank you." The prosecutor sat down.

The jury all turned as one to look at Vivienne, where she sat impassively about four rows of chairs behind the prosecutor's table. I sat on the opposite side of the room to the jury and had a clear view of everyone.

"And what did you understand by the phrase, 'didn't want to lose her,' Sergeant?" Jourdic eyeballed him.

"I don't know. Maybe that he loved her and the husband had come back, and now that was an obstacle to him being with her. Perhaps he meant that it was as if he could now lose her, but did not want to allow that to happen. I don't know exactly."

"Correct. You don't know at all. Do you?" The tone of the questioning was for the first time accusatory rather than probing.

"Well I—"

"Do you know from your own knowledge that your theory is correct?"

"No. No. Not from my own knowledge, but from what I've . . ." he hesitated and stopped.

"Continue, Sergeant Bezart. From what you've heard perhaps. Is that it? Rumour and speculation among the curious and interested citizens of Gigondas and Carpentras and Seguret and Sablet?"

"Well, what I can say about that, is that everyone has a, a . . ."

"A theory? Like yourself, Sergeant. Couldn't Christian Aragon have meant something different from what you thought, as easily as he may have meant what you speculate he intended?"

"Perhaps." The sergeant looked quite demoralised now and considerably less enthusiastic.

"Could he have meant that Madame Pleyben's life was in danger from her husband, and that he feared he might lose her as a consequence of that threat?"

"I don't think he meant that." The sergeant's tone was a shade more confident now that he was expressing an opinion about an opinion, and not a theory about a fact he was unsure of.

"You found another knife at the scene?"

"Yes."

"Belonging to whom?"

"It may have belonged to the deceased."

"*May*? It *may* have belonged to the deceased?"

"I do not know for sure."

"Did he have a sheath on his belt?"

"Yes."

"Did the knife fit that sheath?"

No reply.

"I will repeat my question, Sergeant. Did the knife fit the sheath?"

"Yes." The policeman spoke through his teeth.

"So it *was* his?"

"Possibly."

"Probably?"

"Yes. Probably. But—"

"But what?"

"But it was a long way from the body, and the accused himself was completely unscathed. All of the blood on his hands and clothes came from the deceased." The policeman looked at the jury, as if trying to coax them back to the side of the prosecution.

"So it may have been self-defence?" Jourdic introduced the notion for the first time.

"Yes," said the policeman.

Jourdic smiled and turned to face the jury as he repeated the question. He was now employing the device used by the prosecutor. "It may have been self-defence?"

The jury leaned towards Jourdic ever so slightly, and waited for the confirmation from Sergeant Bezart of the Carpentras Gendarmerie.

"Yes. Monsieur Pleyben may have drawn his knife in self-defence, but it obviously did not save him from having his throat cut and choking on his own blood."

The jury recoiled as one with this new theory to digest. Monsieur Jourdic sat down.

The prosecution called two more witnesses on the first day of the trial. Vernon Pesiere was the crooked concierge at the Hotel St. Saveur. His nose was even longer than I had remembered. He clearly savoured the opportunity to give evidence, and his discernible salivation during his testimony was a mark of his low moral calibre. He gave evidence of renting out two rooms, but only needing to change the bed-clothes in one of them. He heaped his own concern about my welfare onto his sworn information, but it appeared as insincere as it undoubtedly was.

The other witness was the man in the bar at Sablet who had sold George the knife. The man identified George by pointing at him where he sat among the spectators in the courtroom. It was August and baking hot. George was perspiring heavily, and it was impossible to say whether it was the season or the situation that caused him to sweat. Perhaps it was a combination of the two. The witness identified the knife, and then agreed that George had been accompanied by a young man. He nodded in my direction when asked whether that person was present in court.

The prosecutor indicated that he had one more witness, and would call that individual when the court reconvened on the following morning. I was taken back to the Rue du Château, and Monsieur Jourdic came to see me later that evening.

"How do you think it's going?" I asked.

"Not as well as I'd hoped," he replied. "I had expected them to make more of your relationship with Madame Pleyben. At least that might have allowed us not to call her, and to use their own conclusions to drive the jury into the area of crimes of passion. Their decision not to call her character into question in any concerted way, has left the focus of the trial on *you*. I had hoped that the jury might begin to believe that you had been driven by *her* to commit this act of violence. That impression of pressure exerted on your young mind by the older woman might have combined with the self-defence argument to make them unsure as to what exactly happened. In the case of the jury being divided, I think they would acquit you. Our problem now is that we have to make all of those pieces appear ourselves. Both Madame Pleyben and yourself will have to give evidence."

"No, no. We cannot go down that road, Monsieur Jourdic. I do not want her to give evidence. I will not ruin *her* life as well."

"Then—" he shook his old head in a resigned gesture, "—then I am afraid, Christian, you *will* be convicted. You could only have killed this man for a small number of reasons. The jury will be left with a view of only one of those possibilities. You can make the self-defence argument, but I think it is unlikely to succeed. His knife had fallen from his hand before you killed him, yes?"

"Yes. It was already on the floor and out of his reach, but he had held it in his hand—"

"*Before* you drew your own?"

I hesitated and thought for a moment. "No, Monsieur. I know that he certainly seemed to reach for his knife before I drew my own, but it would be untruthful to tell the court that he had drawn it first."

"And that is what you told the police. It is in your statement." Monsieur Jourdic stroked his chin thoughtfully, before an idea appeared to strike him.

"Did you think that he would kill you if you did not kill him?"

"I cannot say that, Monsieur. Of course, it is a real possibility."

"If only you had said *that* in your statement—that what drove you to kill him was a fear for your own life."

"I should have spoken to you before I made the statement."

"It's a little late for that now, Christian. You've also made it clear that Pleyben's knife was out of his reach when you struck with your own."

"What does all this mean, Monsieur?"

"I fear that the cumulative effect of those admissions by you means the jury will be more likely to believe that Pleyben drew it to defend himself against you and not the other way round. Icard will tease out the point and the jury will be left with little choice."

"What should we do then?"

Leopold Jourdic stood up and began to walk up and down the cell talking to himself in a low voice. As he quickened his step, so too did his voice speed up, and his words were now so rushed that I could not decipher them. After many long moments, he turned towards me, and stood over me with his eyes closed for what seemed an eternity. With his eyes still shut, he asked me one more question.

"Are you certain that you do not wish me to call Madame Pleyben to give evidence in your defence?"

"Yes, Monsieur Jourdic. Absolutely certain."

"Then there is only one thing left to do, Christian."

"Yes, Monsieur?"

"You must take the witness stand and plead self-defence. I shall do my very best to save you from the guillotine!"

CHAPTER TEN

Telling the police that Vivienne was not in the house to witness the death of her husband was a deliberate attempt by me to shield her from the trial as much as possible. The prosecution had no real interest in her as a witness. They knew that if they called her to give evidence, she could muddy the water by disclosing facts about her violent marriage. That might sway the jury against the deceased and encourage them to acquit. On the other hand, the prosecution knew there was a risk that Monsieur Jourdic could put her into evidence for the defence, and the information about her violent treatment at the hands of her husband would come out anyway. The difference was that then they would be able to cross-examine her on her relationship with me, and discredit her in that fashion. It was a calculated risk, but for the prosecutor it made more sense to leave her out of it rather than have a hostile witness who might sabotage their case.

Vivienne and I had discussed the matter before she went for the doctor. We agreed that the further she was from the scene at the time of the fatal wounding, the better. Her statement to the police revealed only that she heard a commotion in the house. She said she believed Stephane was venting his anger on her house and her things, instead of on her, and she only returned to the house after it fell silent. In the kitchen she found her husband dead, and her geography pupil bloodstained and in shock. She finished her statement by saying that she imagined I'd had to defend myself, because she knew only too well of her husband's propensity for violence.

Again, it seemed to Monsieur Jourdic that although she had absolutely no basis in fact for saying that she believed her husband to be at fault—because she'd seen nothing of the row—the prosecution would be anxious to avoid this statement getting into the mix of evidence. If they called her, they would be stuck with her statement, whatever its genuine value. In hindsight, perhaps I should have been more careful in my statement, because it seemed that my intimation that the knife was out of his hand at the time Stephane died might now completely undermine the self-defence argument. My response to the threat posed by him had to be commensurate with the threat. Was my life in danger at that moment in time? That is what the members of the jury would have to ask themselves.

If I had said his knife was at my throat first, they would only have had that evidence to test. As it was, I had described the fight in some detail and omitted only that Vivienne was there. I thought that the closer to the truth the statement was, in every other respect, the easier I would find it to be consistent in my evidence if I took the stand.

ON THE morning of the twelfth of August, I awoke at first light and heard the chattering of finches on the window ledge. I saw beside my bed two olives which must have been thrown in during the night. My dreams had hurried in and out of my sleep and I could remember nothing of them. It was warm in the cell and the straw on the floor was thin and wispy, like little hair on an almost-bald man. My clothes were neatly folded on a chair, and I realised that these were clean fresh garments for the second day of my trial. I had supposed that the clean clothes I'd been given the day before would have to be worn throughout the trial. It was a small point, but one which elevated the whole process to a level of humanity I had not expected. I thought about the village and the Dentelles, and for some reason, of Montmirail itself. It was the house where I had been born, and although I'd chosen to reject it along with its inhabitants, I wondered with some fear whether I would ever see it again.

In truth, I know that at that point I wondered if I would ever see the outside world again. Perhaps it was at that moment too that my heart became suffused with fear and regret. Before then, I had never really imagined that I would be convicted and sentenced to death. Now, I imagined the blade of *La Veuve* sliding its metal smile down on the nape of my neck. People say it's over in an instant, but after all, they're not speaking from experience! Before I realised it, I was crying in a strange little way which was a mixture of sobs and breathlessness. I heard the sound of keys in the door in the passageway. I quickly finished dressing and dried my tears. I touched my scar and blessed myself; and for some reason, I imagined Couderc would turn up in court to speak out for me, and tell the world that every experience I'd had with knives had ended badly.

In the courtroom, in the Palais de Justice, the jury box was empty and the public gallery now bristled with even more faces I did not recognise. I spotted my mother in a corner at the back of the court, talking to the lady who owned the bakery in Gigondas—Elise Morel's aunt. I was surprised that Maman had come at all, as I supposed that my father would have forbidden it. My feelings upon seeing her were unclear to me. They were neither warm nor cold, and beyond my surprise, I could not really describe cogent thoughts or emotions concerning her one way or another. I pictured myself standing on the road to Les Florets, looking at Montmirail down two rows of vines where earthy clods of russet soil and stones led like an avenue to my childhood. I had been so eager to grow up and put it all behind me. Now that this had been achieved, I was unsure about what to do next. In the most obvious of ways, this choice had been taken out of my hands. Perhaps the last choice I would ever freely make had been made in the kitchen of my geography teacher's home over a year before.

As we had expected, the last witness for the prosecution was Father Leterrier. He had gained weight in the thirteen months since I'd seen him on the path into the Dentelles below Vivienne's house. His face was more lined than I remembered, and his hands shook slightly from time to time like someone shell-shocked from the war. All in all, he seemed older and more tired. The flare of confidence, which had marked his conversation with me in those last weeks at school, seemed to have all but disappeared. It was impossible to know what had passed through his mind as a result of all of this. I hoped he might feel some responsibility for it.

"You are a member of the community of Jesuits at the Monastery of Crillon-le-Brave?" Monsieur Icard began.

"That is correct." There was a false humility apparent in his eyes, as he replied.

"I think that you teach religion at the lycée where the accused was a pupil until the end of July of last year?"

"That is correct. I have been in sole charge of religious instruction at the lycée in Gigondas for six years. I began work there properly in 1915, after the death of Monsignor Chapus. Before that, I had given occasional talks at the school when the monsignor was away or ill, or when he invited me to speak to a class on a specific topic. At first, I taught in both the boys' and the girls' schools. They have been amalgamated since 1917 because of a shortage of teachers."

"Are you the only provider of religious instruction for the lycée?"

"Yes."

"And can you tell the court and the jury, what is the nature or form of your instruction?"

The priest cleared his throat, and I almost expected him to whisper 'Holy Purity' hoarsely at the prosecutor, but of course he did not.

"I teach each class according to their age and understanding, Monsieur. In the lower years we discuss bible stories, the commandments, the life of Our Lord, the festival of Easter, and we prepare for communion and confirmation—"

"And with the older classes, the children who are preparing to leave the lycée?"

"I teach a range of material dealing with theology and the Apologetics, and of course, I hope for vocations from those older children, to perhaps join the priesthood or the convent."

I thought of his anger at the mention of the story about the Convent of Prebayon and the Devil's Bridge.

"Do you provide any instruction in the area of personal and public morality?"

The prosecutor looked directly across at me for the first time during the trial. The priest looked up at the jury and addressed his answer to them.

"It is quite difficult when you are dealing with adolescents, both boys and girls together, to strike the right balance when instructing them in the subject of morality. One has to be careful, but also, one must not shy away from the responsibility of providing a moral framework for their young lives."

It struck me that in his dealings with my class, Fr. Leterrier had appeared neither careful nor shy in bombarding us with his theories about Holy Purity. Still, I was sure that all of his evidence had been rehearsed with the prosecutor a number of times before. Perhaps the zeal and enthusiasm with which he had imbued his lessons on the subject of sexual morality had been rehearsed out of him.

"But you *do* instruct them about issues of morality?" the prosecutor insisted.

"Yes. Yes, I do. I feel that the short time during which these young people are under my guidance should be used to steel them against the pressures of early adulthood and the temptations of the outside world."

The jury was clearly interested in what the priest had to say.

"Do you know the accused?"

"I knew him by sight as one of my pupils, yes."

"Did you know his name?"

"No. I did not know his name until I made it my business to find it out."

"When and why was that, Father?"

Now the jury was drawn in to the prosecution's case more fully than they could have been on the previous day. The earlier witnesses—apart from the hôtelier—dealt with the mechanics of the death. Now they were being presented with the evidence which could nail down a motive if the prosecutor controlled the priest properly as a witness.

"I saw them on the platform at Avignon."

The information escaped quickly but hung in the air like an arrow in mid-flight. It was clearly an arrow, but it was not yet apparent whether it had a sharp or blunt edge. I suspected the former.

"Now, Father Leterrier, please take your time. What did you see on the platform at Avignon? Perhaps you should tell us first what platform you mean. There are many different platforms, as the jury will know from their own experience. There are platforms in market squares where politicians make speeches, or in theatres where actors play roles. Also, in an execution there is a platform upon which the execution takes place, the convicted person kneeling with their . . ." His voice trailed off.

"The railway station!" Fr. Leterrier exclaimed, like a man who has just solved a riddle.

"Ah, the railway station. At Avignon?"

"Yes, at Avignon. I saw the boy, Aragon, and the widow of Monsieur Pleyben."

"Of course, she was not a widow at that time?" The smile on Monsieur Icard's face indicated to me a belief that things were now going very well for his side of the case. "You saw the accused, and Madame Pleyben. Is that right?"

"Yes."

"On the railway platform at Avignon station?"

"Yes."

"But surely there is nothing unusual about that, Father? They were there as teacher and pupil, on a trip awarded as a prize for a geography project?"

"The only geography I can imagine them learning is that of each other's bodies." Anger was beginning to show in the priest's tone. His eyes began to exhibit the fury and frustration he'd displayed when Elise Morel had rocked her desk a year earlier.

"I don't understand what you mean by that, Father. I am sure my lords and the jury are similarly at a loss." Icard invited the explanation, although it was clear he already knew the answer.

"They were kissing on the platform, Monsieur."

"Kissing?"

"Yes."

"A display of affection and respect, perhaps? A small dusting of the lips on the cheek to say, 'Thank you for your assistance in arranging this educational trip.' Could it not have been that?"

"No. Absolutely not, Monsieur le Prosecutor. They kissed as man and wife, or lovers—passionately, on the mouth and in public. A shameless display of lust and sexual gratification."

"Perhaps you were mistaken, Father?"

"I was not mistaken, Monsieur Icard. The train in which I was travelling came to a rest exactly behind them. As the embrace ended, the boy's face came into view and he observed me in the carriage of the train."

"And what did he do when he saw you?"

"He turned the colour of a setting sun. His face was a clear mixture of shock and embarrassment at being caught in the act of adultery and fornication."

"Are you sure you are not mistaken, Father? I must repeat that possibility to you."

"I have never been more sure of anything. I know what I saw." The priest shook his head for effect and the jury looked over at me. He continued, "I learned later that the other teacher who should have been with them, Monsieur Duchen, he had gone to Paris on . . . business." He spat out the last word.

I could begin to feel my face going red. I looked at Vivienne and she was crying.

"You began before lunch to tell us of your contact with Stephane Pleyben, the deceased. I think you were about to indicate when you first learned of his whereabouts after the war."

"Yes. That is what I was talking about before lunch. I think I had told the court that Stephane had written to me sometime in early 1919. February, perhaps."

"And why did he write to you, Father?"

"It's hard to say. I suppose it was because we knew each other from meeting occasionally in the village before the war. I had come to the school at the invitation of Monsignor Chapus. This was before the schools amalgamated and used the Jesuits' premises exclusively. Once or twice, I'd met Monsieur Pleyben when the school held a celebration dinner at the hotel for the retirement of a teacher, or at graduation ceremonies."

"Did you know him well?"

"No, I hardly knew him at all. But one of the priests at Crillon-le-Brave met him in Bordeaux at a church mission kitchen during the war, and they discussed Gigondas and the school, and of course, he asked about his wife. He would have known then that I was now chaplain to the lycée."

"So what was the purpose of his writing to you?"

"To enquire about his wife, in general terms. He also furnished me with an address where he could be reached if something befell her, or if she needed anything."

"Did the letter speak of anything else?"

"Yes, it did. The letter included details about how he regretted leaving Gigondas and his wife shortly after the war had commenced. He said he longed to return, but knew that the military authorities might want to talk to him about having missed out on conscription."

"Do you have the letter still?"

"Yes. I have it here." The priest rummaged in a small cloth bag tied to the rope around his waist. The letter was shown to the judges and to Monsieur Jourdic, and then to the jury.

"When did you next have a communication with Monsieur Pleyben?"

"After confronting the boy and Madame Pleyben and receiving no satisfactory response from either of them, I wrote to him. Despite being given the chance to be truthful about the affair and to end it, neither of them appeared prepared to take the necessary steps."

"So you wrote to Monsieur Pleyben?"

"I did."

"And when you wrote, what did you tell him?"

"I informed him of his wife's infidelity. I urged him to return to Gigondas to save his marriage, her soul, and the entire life and future of an innocent young boy."

Monsieur Icard allowed the import of the last phrase to sink into the jury's subconscious. One man looked over at me with a degree of sympathy I had not detected before. The priest continued testifying about meeting Monsieur Pleyben at the train station in Violes, and bringing him to Gigondas where they confronted Vivienne together.

"Can you tell the jury what the mood of that meeting was, Father?"

"Yes, I can truthfully say that although it was a great surprise for Madame Pleyben, I detected a willingness in her voice and demeanour to consider the long-term benefit of a reconciliation. I had already spoken on Monsieur Pleyben's behalf to the military authorities in Orange. I hoped he might simply be reprimanded or fined, or perhaps engaged by the army for some period performing manual work, as a sanction for not having obeyed his conscription orders. The mood had softened somewhat I think, and there has been great debate about the manner in which the war was conducted; so perhaps leniency was a real possibility."

"In any event, Monsieur Pleyben was prepared to face those consequences, be they harsh or lenient, in order to save his marriage?"

"Undoubtedly, Monsieur. Undoubtedly."

"You left Monsieur and Madame Pleyben alone?"

"Yes. I had warned Stephane to be patient with her and not to expect too much too soon. I knew it might be difficult for both of them, but I was greatly optimistic as a result of their reaction to each other after the initial surprise."

I looked down at Vivienne. She was shaking her head silently.

"You left?"

"As soon as the introductions had been completed, I left."

"Did you detect anger in the attitude of Monsieur Pleyben?"

"Certainly not. He was worried, of course, about having been away for so long. He was concerned about the military, what people in the village would think. But this was, in my opinion, a natural reaction to the situation."

"In her statement to the police, Madame Pleyben spoke of difficulties they had had in their time together before he left Gigondas. Did anyone ever speak to you about this? Did you ever observe anything which evidenced this?"

"No, I cannot say that I did, but all marriages have problems, Monsieur Icard. The plan of God is that people work together to overcome those 'difficulties,' as you call them. Our Lord expects us to face temptations resolutely, and that is how we defeat them."

Sensing a morality lecture, Monsieur Icard steered the priest back on track. I wondered why he had mentioned

Vivienne's marital problems. I concluded that it was a pre-emptive strike in case she was called for the defence, since Icard would have no witnesses to contradict her evidence. He was trying to counter that possibility by using the priest's testimony in a subtle way that could be used in the closing speech to rebut any of her evidence about Stephane's mal-treatment. If Vivienne was not called, then the issue was not properly opened to the jury and posed no threat to Icard's case. He was a very clever lawyer despite his apparently casual approach to the examination of his witnesses.

"Did you meet anyone on your way back to the village?"

"Yes, I met young Aragon."

"The accused?"

"Yes."

"Where?"

"On the pathway down to the village, just above the hos-pice and the graveyard."

"Did you speak?"

"Yes, we did have a brief conversation, yes."

"What did you speak about?"

"I told him to turn back from his journey. I meant, Mon-sieur, both in the physical and moral sense."

"Yes. Continue. Did he respond? Did the accused say anything?"

"I'm afraid he did, Monsieur."

"Can you recall, Father, what it was he said?"

Father Leterrier shook his finger in the general direction of the people present, as though warning them in advance never to say whatever it was he was about to recount.

"He threatened that he would kill me if I continued to interfere in their lives."

A silence descended over the entire room. Everybody, except me, looked shocked.

I looked at the priest and shouted, "This is not true. That's not what I said."

I stood up, but was restrained by a prison warder who forced me to sit down.

Monsieur Icard turned slowly to face me head-on, his back to the jury, as if he were their commander and they a small band of soldiers on a march. "You will have ample opportunity to tell everybody your side of the story. If you choose to."

Monsieur Jourdic was incensed and made an immediate objection to the remark. He spoke of the adverse inference that the prosecutor was trying to insinuate if I did not give evidence. The judges were not on our side; the presiding judge made that clear.

"If the accused chooses not to give evidence then, of course, no adverse inference can be drawn, Monsieur Jourdic. But neither will we permit unsworn testimony to be shouted from the benches."

I knew I shouldn't have spoken out, but it's bloody hard to shut up when your neck is at stake.

"You are sure about what he said?" Icard spoke in an off-hand manner to emphasise my transgression.

"I am sure of it; and what is more, Monsieur, I must confess that from his words and his eyes, I believed him."

"Did you believe that Madame and Monsieur Pleyben would be reconciled?"

"I did, and I can say that nothing has happened to move me from that view."

"The death of Monsieur Pleyben was the event which prevented that reconciliation?"

"Obviously," the priest said, in a tired tone.

Most people in the room smiled at this rare moment of levity.

Jourdic was brief in his cross-examination.

"You were outraged by what you perceived as the affair between Christian Aragon and Madame Pleyben?"

"I was concerned and worried about the welfare of both parties." The priest looked smug.

"You were concerned enough to confront both of them separately, and threaten them."

"I warned them, yes. I felt that I had an obligation to intervene and to deflect them from the path of—"

"Evil?"

"If you like. Their relationship was an affront to God and to the community."

"So, you took matters into your own hands and contacted the conscription-avoiding husband who had deserted his country—and his wife—at a time when at least his country wanted him?"

Icard rose to his feet. "I presume that if a slur is going to be cast on the character of the deceased as regards his treatment of Madame Pleyben, then Madame Pleyben will be called to give evidence of this?"

The senior presiding judge looked down at Jourdic and raised his eyebrows.

"I will not be calling any evidence in that regard, My Lords."

I saw the clear shadow of a smile pass over the visage of Monsieur Icard. He sat down and looked over at the jury as he did, undoubtedly conveying to them his assessment of the significance of the public defender's statement.

"Could you have misheard Christian Aragon, Father Leterrier? Could he have perhaps indicated that if *you* had harmed Madame Pleyben, then he would make you accountable?"

"No, Monsieur. There is no reason why he should have believed that I might harm her. I am certain that it was in the context of his seeing me as interfering in their relationship."

"You were simply trying to help?" Jourdic smirked.

"Yes."

"By bringing back her husband, after six years, to effect a reconciliation?"

"Yes. I have already said that."

"But your aim was to disrupt the liaison, that of Madame Pleyben and Christian Aragon. No?"

"My aim was, and let me be very clear about this, my aim was to effect a reconciliation. To restore the marital unit so that it could continue and prosper. That was my principal purpose, Monsieur!" The priest was ebullient now.

"Then, please tell the court and the jury, Father, why you did not take any steps for the seventeen months, between February 1919 and July 1920, to bring about this reconciliation, your *principal* purpose?"

The priest was silent.

"Two further questions, Father. You brought Monsieur Pleyben to Gigondas by yourself. No one else knew of his arrival in Gigondas in July, 1920?"

"That is correct."

"So, when Monsieur Icard said in his opening speech that the murder was planned 'down to the last detail,' he cannot be correct can he? Christian Aragon could not have known about the return of Monsieur Pleyben until he reached the house and found it out for himself?"

"I suppose not." The priest finally looked defeated.

"No more questions, My Lords," said Monsieur Jourdic.

"The prosecution's case has finished," said Monsieur Icard, with a little less confidence in his tone.

CHAPTER ELEVEN

I was overwhelmed with gratitude and surprise when George Phavorin was called as the first witness in my defence. Monsieur Jourdic had told me nothing in advance about it, and I suppose his instinct in that regard had been right. Had I known I would have urged George, with all of my heart, to stay away from my trial. The taint of loyalty to me might damage his standing at Montmirail where his future livelihood and lodgings were at my father's discretion. I could not bring that down upon him. However, he was a good witness and he lent to my defence a fresh sprinkling of humanity and honesty that I could see appealed to the jury.

"Have you ever known Christian Aragon to be violent?" Jourdic asked.

"Never."

"Are you quite sure about that?"

"Yes, Monsieur. I am. I have known Christian for a long time, since he was a young boy of four or five, and in all that time I have never seen him raise his hand to anyone."

"You bought this for him?" Jourdic held up the knife, and I could see him closing the blade deliberately and slowly into the handle, trying to convey an image of an implement capable of indolence as well as activity.

"Yes. We were at the market at Sablet and I offered to buy it for him."

"Had you gone to the market for the specific purpose of buying the knife?"

"No, not at all. I was delivering wine to the train and we went into the bar for a drink. The man who sold it to me was there also. I think he'd been in the market all morning."

"Did Christian Aragon ask you to buy the knife for him?"

"No, Monsieur. He did not. I offered to buy it as a gift for him."

"Thank you, Monsieur Phavorin. I have no further questions."

Monsieur Icard rose from his seat with an air of someone who was weary and anxious for a boring conversation at a party to end. He looked at me and then at George.

"You are fond of Christian Aragon?" This was the first time he'd used my name.

"He is a great friend. Yes."

"And the son of your employer?"

"Yes."

"You feel affection and respect for Christian?"

"Yes."

"And loyalty?"

"Naturally."

"You bought him the knife?"

"Yes. I have agreed already with Monsieur Jourdic on that point. You see—"

"You did not know what he was going to do with the knife?"

"How do you mean?"

"I mean that when you purchased the knife you had no sinister motive for doing so?"

"Of course not."

"And you imagined that it would be used for—" He paused. "To skin rabbits perhaps, or to carve wood?"

"Perhaps those kinds of things. Yes."

"But you never imagined it might be used to kill a man? To puncture his throat? To make a spray of blood spurt into the air over his face, and to splatter on the stone floor of his own home?"

"What do you mean, Monsieur?"

"I mean, Monsieur Phavorin, that you never imagined that your gift would be put to that use. Did you?"

"Of course, I didn't. I never for a moment believed that it would play any part in . . . in any of the things you said!" George was quite shaken by the questioning, and it was hard to say whether it was the topic of discussion or the manner of delivery of the questions that disturbed him most.

Icard paused. "But it did play such a part, did it not?"

"I don't know whether it did or not." George's tone was defensive now.

"Oh surely, Monsieur Phavorin, you have heard the evidence of the prosecution witnesses, Sergeant Bezart and the doctor?"

"No, Monsieur. I did not hear their evidence. I was not here."

"I apologise, Monsieur Phavorin. It was unfair of me to assume that you had been here for their evidence. Of course, you could have no idea of what either of them said if you were not here when they gave that evidence. Please accept my apology for that presumption."

"Of course, Monsieur." George straightened up a little in the witness chair and began to look more assured.

"And on the twenty-sixth of July of last year, at about three o'clock in the afternoon, where were you?"

"Working in the four hectares belonging to my employer, above the church. I was clearing them of rabbits."

"How long were you working there?" Icard looked at his fingertips, as if bored with his own questions.

"All day, Monsieur. I had lunch at Montmirail at midday, and returned to my work until sunset."

"Presumably then, if you were not there, you can have absolutely no idea of what transpired at the house of Madame Pleyben on that same afternoon?"

Icard looked up from his nails and I saw a sneer creep over his face as he glared at George. It was a look of arrogant triumph, and it was the first time it appeared to me that the prosecutor had a personal interest in the outcome of my trial. I feared for George, and felt that he was about to be discredited in his efforts just when I needed his assistance most. I need not have been afraid.

"Were you there, Monsieur Icard? Was the doctor there during the altercation? Was Sergeant Bezart there?"

The jury sat up as one and leaned out into the room, engaged by this small act of defiance. The prosecutor moved to quell the challenge.

"How dare you address me like that, Monsieur? I am asking the questions here. You are a witness for the defence, and your function at this time is to answer my questions. Not to ask your own."

Icard sought the support of the judges to trample down this insubordination, but it was not forthcoming. The tension between the two men began to rise, as the prosecutor sought to retake the advantage in their exchange.

"I shall repeat my question, Monsieur. How can you have any information to offer the court about what happened on that afternoon, in that house, when you were not there yourself?"

George paused, but only for an instant. "Let me say this in answer to your question, Monsieur Icard. Do we have to be outside to know that it is raining? We can hear the sound of the drops on the roof when we are half-asleep. We may hear nothing at all, and wake the following day to find the countryside wet and the water barrels full, we—"

"Answer the question." The prosecutor's voice rose now, and his hands fumbled aimlessly through papers on the table in front of him.

"If you will allow me the opportunity, Monsieur. I may not have your education, or your eloquence, but—"

"ANSWER THE QUESTION!" Icard roared at George.

I thought for a moment that he was going to climb over the table and into the witness stand and shake the life out of him.

"Please control yourself, Monsieur Icard," the presiding judge's voice cut across the argument like a bucket of cold water on two frisky dogs.

Icard glowered at George, who smiled at him; then Jourdic rode to the rescue like one of the musketeers, raising himself halfway between sitting and standing.

"My Lords, can the witness be permitted to answer without being bullied by Monsieur Icard?" The tone of suggestion was just right, and it had the effect of widening the crack in the proceedings to a size that would allow George to continue.

"I am sure that Monsieur Icard has regained his customary composure now," said the judge to the left of the presiding one. "Please continue, Monsieur Phavorin."

No further interruption could have been countenanced; this solitary intervention from a new voice was final in its authority. George glanced at me and then at the jury, and he took a sip of water from a glass offered to him by the court clerk. He began again and we all listened, even Monsieur Icard, until he had finished.

"I do not have to be everywhere to know anything. I want you to imagine your own lives, and the things that you believe, but which you have not witnessed with your own eyes. Every single day we accept the word of others who have borne witness to things which are mundane or exciting or frightening. We know people who fought at Verdun and the Marne; we accept their accounts of the horror from which they protected us. We *know* from our history."

He laughed. "What do we know? A man comes home with one arm, and says that while fighting the Germans a shell blew it off in a trench filled with water and rats and rotting corpses. Do we challenge his story? No. We believe him because he said that he was there, and that this is how it happened. Do we say to him, 'You must be lying' or, 'Are you sure?' Perhaps he was running away from the front lines, or helping the enemy, and maybe something like an accident happened. If we *know* that man, if he is our friend or our brother or our son, we know whether he is lying. We are so quick to judge, to say it must have been this way or that way, when we have not seen it ourselves.

"Monsieur le Prosecutor, I can tell you that I know this man, this boy, the accused. I have known him for most of his life and for a large part of my own. I know that if he had sought out the deceased, Monsieur Pleyben, to kill him deliberately, then you would have no need for this trial because Christian Aragon would have pleaded guilty. Whatever happened on that afternoon in that house at that precise time, you are correct, I did *not* witness it myself. Nevertheless, I *can* tell you something of what happened, because I *do* know one of the two men who were there: Christian Aragon. He may have had a knife, he may have had blood on his hands, but he is not a murderer. I do not think that he has murder in his heart.

"If Christian Aragon killed this man, then it was not because he murdered him in cold blood. 'Self-preservation,' 'provocation,' I do not know what words you lawyers use to convey this absence of intent to kill for its own sake. I do not care about theories and assumptions and the trail of blood-stained clothes. I know the boy and he is not a murderer. I do not have to be everywhere to know anything, and I most certainly do not need to have been there in that house at that time to know this."

My eyes were streaming with tears as the room fell silent. I felt the weight of attention that warns you people are looking at you when you cannot see them. Nothing in my life had ever prepared me for this moment when I could feel such tidal waves of admiration and inadequacy for being the recipient of such a grand gesture of support and love from a fellow human being. The jury was still quiet, but some of them were scribbling notes on the papers before them that until then had remained blank. It was the most extraordinary moment in my entire life, and for a minute or two everything was silent and at one with my spirit. All I could hear was the beating of my own heart. I saw Monsieur Icard lean across the desk towards Jourdic. They spoke for a moment in whispers. Jourdic then got to his feet and addressed the court.

"I wonder if My Lords would be so obliged as to allow us a short period of time for consultation?"

The judges nodded and rose, and the room rose with them. They left the court, walking slowly behind the clerk to the curtain which covered the door to their chambers.

"LET ME explain to you what's happened here." Leopold Jourdic gripped my arms to emphasise how serious things had become. We were alone in a small room with the door ajar.

"I'm listening, Monsieur."

"This is extraordinary, Christian. I've never seen anything like it before."

His eyes were like that of a child seeing snow for the very first time: all bright and wide and excited.

"Like what before? Never seen anything like what?" I was still overwhelmed with emotion, completely in the dark.

"Icard is worried about the jury. He thinks that after your friend George's performance, there is a very real chance that they might acquit you."

"That's good, isn't it?" I could see a prison guard outside the door.

"Yes. Yes, of course it is. But it may not be good for very long."

"I don't understand this, Monsieur."

"All right. Here is how things stand at the moment. Icard is concerned that you might be acquitted on the charge of murder, so he is prepared to offer another, lesser charge, if you will plead guilty."

"Why should I plead guilty at this stage? We're only beginning my defence now. Isn't that correct?"

"Yes, that's true. But *you* are going to give evidence next. You will be asked about the knife, the one the deceased had. Your statement says it was out of his hand before you struck with your own."

"That is correct."

Jourdic was beginning to sweat now. The room itself was warm, and only one tiny barred window gave any natural light to the situation. He continued.

"If you give evidence, you will be asked about his knife and where it was when you killed him. If you say it was away from him, and therefore no threat to you, then you will not be believed when we maintain that it was self-defence."

"And if I say something different?"

"For example?"

"If I say I don't remember, or I'm not sure now where it was. Or I could say I was sure *he* was going to kill *me* if I did not take his life first."

"Then you will be lying and I cannot allow you to do that. Unless of course you were lying when you made your statement, and you're telling the truth about it now. But it makes no sense that you wouldn't have told the police the knife was in his hand and you feared for your own life when you made your statement. Either way, the statement will be before the jury. I am sure that Icard will convince them in his closing argument that it was not self-defence."

"But why does *he* fear an acquittal if *you* are so certain that I will be convicted, Monsieur?" It made no sense to me that they could be so divided in their views.

"Because—" he smiled a wide grin, "—because of George Phavorin and his dramatic speech. Icard now feels under threat from the defence and is thinking not logically, but emotionally. For the moment at least he is seeing the jury and not the evidence as the most important piece in this puzzle. I think that our case, such as it is, is at its highest point now."

"What will happen if I plead guilty to a lesser charge? What is the charge?"

"Unlawful killing. The benefit for you is that it does not automatically carry the death penalty. That is up to the judges. If you plead guilty, it is almost impossible to imagine them sending you to the guillotine. Given your age and a guilty plea, I think you will only get a prison sentence."

"How long would that be?" I thought of my cell on the Rue du Château. Could I imagine it as my home?

"The maximum is life imprisonment, but I think somewhere between ten and twenty years is probably what you'd get."

Twenty years? I was only seventeen years old now!

"The court is about to resume, gentlemen." A clerk with a black gown spoke to us through the open door.

I felt the weight of my whole life bearing down on my head like a wood press. A whole rhapsody of mistakes and choices had conspired to bring me to that point, and I was in no condition to properly evaluate the options now being presented. I thought of Vivienne, of my brother Eugene, of Couderc, and for some reason, of the woman with the basket on the bridge in Avignon. My soul leaped about in that tiny room, and I felt the walls close in and try to catch it. I could hardly think straight, let alone speak.

"We must give them an answer, Christian." Jourdic's voice quavered in the heat and the situation.

"What should I do, Monsieur?" I held my hands out like a beggar and hoped that somehow I would not have to make the decision myself.

Monsieur Jourdic stood back and eyed me as if I were his own flesh and he was hemorrhaging lifeblood with me in this crisis, at an equal rate.

"The rest of your life is outside this room, waiting for you. Try to make the distance between now and the end of it as great as possible."

The door behind my lawyer opened fully and we were beckoned back to the court, with prison warders and policemen in their heavy flannel uniforms almost staggering in the heat.

"Alright, then." I gasped in the August air from the space between us, and took my destiny into my own hands. "Guilty it is."

CHAPTER TWELVE

My incarceration ended on the twenty-fourth day of October, 1936. It was a hard and cruel time. I was lucky in some respects to have managed to survive without gaining more serious injuries—both visible and unseen—than the ones I had accumulated during that time. A trail of years behind me led from the Palais de Justice in Carpentras to the nearby prison; and eventually, on a cold February night in 1922, to the notorious confines of the small but inhospitable Prison Caisserie in the shadow of the remains of the Église des Accoules in Marseille. It was never explained to me why I was moved from Carpentras, but I guessed it may have been to put some considerable distance between Vivienne and myself, so as to make visiting more difficult for her. If someone was hoping to sever the bonds between us by this crass act of bureaucracy, they failed utterly.

Prison is like an animal, a wolf perhaps, which creeps into your garden at night and demands attention. You have to decide from the earliest time possible how you are going to treat it. Will you let it stalk you and lie in wait for you and advance each evening? If you do that, or try to do that, you will find that no matter how much you believe you have placated it, it always returns; and each time it is bigger and stronger and even more difficult to face. Eventually, it will kill you, or more likely perhaps, it will drive you to perform that task yourself.

"Is this your first time inside?" asked an inmate called Lautrec in Prison Caisserie, as he approached me with his cup held out in front of him for my ration of thin watery soup. It was two days after my transfer to Marseille. All around us, prisoners huddled in twos and threes, their faces a mix of fear and nervous complicity. This was my test. I had heard from one of the jailors in Carpentras that life in Marseille would be very different indeed. He addressed his remarks to a location below my waist.

"They'll like you down there, in Marseille." He smirked at his double meaning. "You'll have to find out very quickly who does what to make sure you stay alive."

I felt myself begin to shake as Lautrec's cup clanked against mine. There was a hue of excitement around us, and some men began to nudge each other. Others sniggered. I thought about George and of his courage in defending me in court. I had to keep my mind on being free again someday, and to do that I had to stay alive. The animal was in my garden and I was being forced to make a choice. The cups clanged again.

"You are very kind, Monsieur. To offer to share your soup with me," I said. Lautrec stopped short and looked around at the others with a cackle.

"I'm offering *him* am I?"

There was a loyal laugh from the huddle around us. He turned his face to mine and rattled the cups again, this time tipping his own towards me so that I could see that it was empty. Now he grew in confidence and turned his enamel receptacle upside down, so the watching world too would know that it was empty. Our eyes met, and I saw that behind his green pupils the slightest hesitation was hopping about amongst vast reserves of violence.

"This *must* be your first time inside, friend, because you don't understand the rules. *You* are the one who is going to show the kindness by giving me *your* ration."

The audience shuffled a little more easily, now that their leader was reasserting his control over them through me.

I smiled and bowed my head in submission. "Of course, Monsieur. The error is mine." I reached out my left hand and took his empty cup from him. As slowly and as carefully as

I could, I poured my ration into it. Not a drop was spilled and when the transfer was complete, I handed his cup back to him.

Lautrec raised his secondhand soup in a toast to his subjects. As they cheered, he began to drink.

"AArgGhaCHAG."

Lautrec half-gargled and yelled as I slammed my right palm against the base of the cup as he gorged. The brittle edge of the tired pocked-white enamel cut into his mouth and forced his face back up into the light, which fell weakly into the dining area through two narrow slits halfway up the wall. He screamed and bled, shaking like a stuck boar. Everyone else in the room seemed to be drawn in to us, and yet stopped short as though an invisible fence surrounded that moment, the man and this boy. As the jailors flailed their way through that manacled mass, I knew that this animal called 'prison' was still in my garden and needed more attention. I wrenched the cup from Lautrec's red pumping face, and held it aloft in a fresh toast to these people I had only recently met. As the jailors rained blows on me through the crowd, I lifted the cup to my own lips and drained the horror-draught of blood and soup. The animal might return to my garden each evening, but it would have to wait sometimes until I was ready to feed it.

Even now, at this remove, I do not know what possessed me to respond as I did. My early childhood had been the scene of repeated beatings by my father, and yet I had never struck him. I had not hesitated to come to the assistance of Vivienne when I came upon the situation in which she was being attacked by her husband. In that struggle I had defended my own life from threat also. But this was the first time I'd ever pre-empted violence with aggression of my own. I can only imagine that at that one moment all of my fears and experiences fused into an understanding. It was a recognition that the certain consequence of appeasement in prison was to be cowed by the threat of others to the point

137

where my own life would have been worth nothing. I knew that I had to face the fear or else drown in it.

I was devoured from the inside out by my passion and love for Vivienne Pleyben. Those feelings carried me out of myself and my pain and horror whenever salvation was required during that time. Much like my dream-flights as a child and a young man, it felt like an external force capable of lifting me to a place of calm in times of peril. The combination of the 'Enamel Episode,' and my love for Vivienne gave me the protection I needed in order to endure the heat and the cold of prison. For the most part, I was left alone.

My heart had not known when I was sixteen what lay ahead. My designs for life were, I admit, fashioned from negativity: from a desire not to inherit Montmirail, not to replace Eugene in my father's future, not to be shackled by the smallness of Gigondas itself. All of those aims had disappeared in the short time between the trip to Avignon and my being sentenced to thirty years for unlawful killing—with a recommendation that I serve at least fifteen.

Any chance of succumbing to the expectations of others was destroyed in that small house at the foot of the Dentelles on the day I graduated from school. The view of the peaks that towered over the village, with its red roofs and chapel bell-tower and fever hospice and mayor's residence, was changed forever on that afternoon. I became the focus of the village and its people for a time.

What about the teacher? Where were his parents during the trial? Did you hear of how they boasted about eating chocolates in Avignon? All of these unanswered questions, and the thousands of insinuations those questions were midwives for, kept that little place in Provence going for a decade. It was like petrol for people. The scenes of our story, the locations of its constituent elements, became like a series of shrines for locals and inquisitive visitors alike. I could not have cared less. My part in the drama had afforded me a purpose in life, and I had been allowed to move offstage to catch my breath. Now, a decade and a half later, I had truly caught it.

Vivienne had left the village a couple of weeks after the trial, and lodged in Orange for eighteen months or so in a pension on the Rue Lacourt. She sold her house to Vaton for a fair price and used the money to be close by me, and to survive. It might have rained apples and pears on alternating days for all I knew of the outside world. But her visits to me in prison kept me sane and gave me something to live for. When I was moved to Marseille, Vivienne once again made her own arrangements to be near me. She eventually found work in a small school on the Rue Sylvabelle where the pay was poor, but the past was not an issue. My days and nights were filled to capacity with longing and desire for her. No amount of discouragement concealed in the intensity of prison life deflected me from the belief that we would eventually be reunited and make a life together.

For her part, I must say that she spoke invariably in positive and encouraging terms during her visits and in her letters. I could not have been surprised, at any time, if she had ceased to visit, stopped writing, or simply announced that she could not wait for me until France was ready to disgorge me from its prison system. None of these things happened. Our feelings for each other remained strong and grew in an intensity which sought to compensate for the lack of physical intimacy, by committing each day and hour and moment to the other. The hardship of prison life and the unwanted attentions of the system itself, did nothing to approach breaking me or weakening my resolve or my heart.

"How are things in the school?" I would always ask first when she visited.

"Fine, fine," she would answer. "And how are you?" Vivienne would enquire even when my face bore bruises and gashes. Sometimes our words were accurate and valid, and our exchanges carried real news across the table. Mostly though our hearts spoke and our tongues prattled to give our hearts some privacy. There were no words adequate to say what we needed to.

In the summer of 1936, I was informed by Monsieur Jourdic's office that the Board of the Southern Prison Authority had considered my case and recommended my release. Taking into account the period of imprisonment before trial, it added up to a total of slightly more than sixteen years. I had spent almost exactly half of my life behind bars.

In the weeks and days before my sentence ended, Vivienne was allowed more liberal visiting opportunities, and we spoke of where we would go and what we were likely to do. I must say that all of those conversations had about them a hue of unreality, as we both feared that the recommendation for release might be withdrawn or overturned by some appeal mechanism open to the state.

Vivienne had applied for a job in Biarritz and was accepted. Our plan was to go there if I was released before the end of October. The teaching position would start on November first when the current employee would be leaving. The post was as a private tutor to the daughter of a family that had made their fortune in government bonds during the war. It carried a modest enough remuneration, but also a small home, free of rent, on the Rue Verlaine.

The harsh buffeting of the coast and the infectious laughter of rain on the roof serenaded our reunion, and they are sounds I shall love forever. Vivienne was forty when I left prison, and yet we were like teenagers together, making love with a mixture of passion and gratitude which left us both at once tired, satisfied, and eager to recommence.

I do not mean to trivialise the years that interrupted our lovemaking. Of course, they had ripped us apart in an instant and had left any hopefulness to ourselves to create. They weakened our bodies in the way that age must, but they did not dent our resolve or our affection. You may not believe me, because we are all products of our own experiences, but there is nothing in this world as forceful or unrelenting as the love of two people who are prepared to wait for each other. When I was sixteen my life was a torrent of fog and mist and no clear way led anywhere that I could see. In that same period beyond sixteen, my whole existence and life and purpose became as clear as crystal. Doctors, lawyers, politicians, soldiers, undertakers, and bakers—they are all necessary and noble professions. But no vocation approaches the vitality and importance of that most exalted of callings: to love and to be loved in return. If my entire time in prison had served only the purpose of ensuring the opportunity to spend another five minutes with Vivienne, then it would have been infinitely worthwhile. My philosophy had become one of love and sacrifice, each completely justifying the other. The rest is just idle talk and overdone croissants.

Of course, there were parts of my life in prison I could never share with Vivienne. I think everybody carries small boxes within them, which they alone may open to view the contents. The barbarian in me could never be with her and be accepted. I am pretty sure of that. She would never understand—or would she? In any event, there are pieces of all of us which we cannot expect others to accept or understand. Life, though, is sometimes kind enough to allow the boy who carried the box in which the barbarian lives, to be loved.

My MOTHER died in 1929. It was never clear to me what had caused her death—I suspected suicide—but I understood from George that her last years had been lonely and black.

"Your mother did not leave the house after your trial," he told me, on one of his visits to see me in prison in Marseille.

"And my father?"

"He has withdrawn into himself, now. He rarely speaks at all, except to order me around or to complain about the harvest."

"He was always an expert when it came to complaining," I said, with a smile.

George's visits were rare, although he wrote regularly and I wrote back. I addressed the letters to him at the *Notaire*'s office. I did not want to make life for him at Montmirail any more difficult than it must have been after he had appeared at the trial. He made the long trip to see me to tell me of my mother's death, and to save me from hearing of it in some other way. I have no doubt, and there can objectively be none, that he saved my life and that is the short answer to all of that.

Sometimes in July, when my father continued to travel to Paris in search of the *Medaille d'Or*, George would use that time to visit me. He continued to live in the gate-lodge on the road to Les Florets, and he was almost seventy when I was released. I wrote to him every month, and he gave us his blessing when I told him that Vivienne and I were to be married in Biarritz. I asked him to come and visit us there, but he said that he doubted whether he could travel that far, given his age. He wrote letters in a hand that continued to fail steadily.

Robert Aragon pursued his dream of the great prize in Paris, even after my mother died. I discovered later from George that my father did not shed a single tear at her funeral. How she had continued to live with him and follow his steps around that house with food and love is hard to understand. Perhaps I, of all people, should have been able to comprehend that kind of indefatigable devotion, but I must confess that it was utterly beyond me. That house died when Eugene was killed, and in a way, my father became soulless on that date too. I was a poor substitute for Eugene and the promise of greatness he held out in my father's eyes.

George was one reason perhaps why I should have returned to Gigondas upon my release. Maybe if I had searched my heart there would have been other, more obvious draws back to the village of my birth. It was the only other place I had ever lived apart from prison. Why did I not hanker to pay my respects at my mother's resting place in the village cemetery? Or long to feel the dust on my feet from the track above the fever hospice which had led me to my destiny? I cannot really say. But it was as though the greater part of me had said goodbye to all of that years earlier, when I knew that I was going to leave anyway. That is what I told myself, at any rate.

And my father, what about him? I know that you may well look at my life and think this and that about my choices, but perhaps even I too accept that in one respect my business in Gigondas was unfinished. My grand plan to declare my love for Vivienne upon his return from Paris in July, 1920, was still unexecuted. My great hope of being open and adult about my feelings for her, or my expectation of hearing the rebukes or sneers that would have been my father's response, never came to be played out. I wanted so much to break free decisively from his control, and yet that planned moment of confrontation had never transpired. Perhaps that was for the best. Maybe all breaking of chains should be quiet.

I was lifted out of that place by romance, by blood and death and criminality and justice and revenge. The game had progressed from the original rules to a plateau way above all of us, which we could only stretch to reach and feel about with our hands, seeking to make some sense of the things we touched. But I couldn't get my father out of my mind. *Why did you not attend the trial? What is it about you that drew loyalty from my mother? Did you know that I could never even try to fill the void Eugene left in everyone's life, including my own?* These were the questions I might have asked had I returned to Montmirail upon leaving prison. It was not the case that I had never formulated those questions in my mind, because I had almost every hour of every day. No, I think that the lure of the past had diminished, and I wanted to look ahead instead of behind.

That house could have been mine if I had stayed and never got involved in matters of the heart. Families are the great marketplace, where all members barter and trade on an ongoing basis, sometimes for great loss and little gain. From the moment we kick our way into them, families demand all sorts of bargains from us and we from them. No argument or silence or caress or compliment comes free of charge. There is always a price to pay, and sooner or later the debt is called in or the credit note cashed. No one counts their change quite like a blood relative. The price I would have had to pay to inherit Montmirail would have been enormous. I would have had to walk so closely behind my father that I would've had to become part shadow in order to survive. Of necessity, I could not have even contemplated a relationship with Vivienne. I would have been nudged in the direction of some local girl with the background and outlook that most closely coincided with my father's. I would have had to behave in a predictable, safe way in order to earn either his respect or my inheritance. It was, in my view, too high a price to pay for one's own destruction. Eugene was the only one who could have filled the shoes that he himself had left behind; my feet were either too small or too cold. That entire place, with its granite pudding rocks and ancient cellars and tired winepresses and expensive delft, was now not mine by choice. The history within Montmirail's walls and windows owed me nothing, nor I it.

"I LOVE you," I whispered and shouted and called and mimed to Vivienne a thousand times a day after my release. She echoed those words so frequently it was impossible to keep count of who spoke them or how often in any given period of time. It mattered little because we were together, and each moment spent in each other's company was a gift.

"Did you ever think of giving up hope?" she would ask.

"Never," I would reply.

"Not once?"

"Not even once. And you, did you ever consider for a moment that you would be unable to wait or that I might never be released?"

"Never," she would reply. "Not once."

I have to live with the consequences of my actions. My hands never did anything I had not asked them to. I am shocked by the brutality of which people are capable. Yes, I do mean that. I do mean that my own moments of madness shock me on some level. To avoid solitary confinement in the Prison Caisserie during one particularly harsh winter, I held lighted cigarettes against the palm of my hand for ten minutes, while my captors made wagers on how long I would last.

How can I explain this to you, in language which does not appear either too weak or too forceful, what it means to love and to be separated and to reunite? It is to have in your hand a piece of sunshine. That sunshine is snatched away and you are left with black ashes in your palm. One day, in the most unexpected fashion, you bathe your skin in apparently filthy water, and when you draw out your arm, angels appear on each one of your fingers and remain there forever. This is exactly what it is like.

THE ONE place from my family's past which I had resolved to visit was the site where Eugene met his death. I made the trip to the ghostly quiet ruin of Fort Douaumont some months after my release. The story of its ultimate collapse and of how easily it occurred made me sad for Eugene. A Lieutenant Radtke and Captain Haupt virtually stole the fort from the French forces with a handful of men. Eugene was one of the many soldiers who died in that manoeuvre, and I must say that I often question the sanity of his fighting for France when France was apparently so ill-equipped to protect him during that struggle. Wars are the public display of private uncertainty—that now seems clear. I met veterans of the Great War in prison and many of them regretted ever getting involved. They were the rabbits in the lantern light, while the men who made the light shine stayed in the shadows.

On that excursion, I do not know how close I may have walked to where my brother fell; but what mattered to me was that I had physically gotten as close to him as I could given my limited knowledge of the area and the regeneration of the ground beneath my feet.

VIVIENNE AND I married in January, 1937, a month after my visit to the battlefield where Eugene had died and was buried. The Popular Front Government had come to power months earlier, and it really seemed as if politically, at least, France had turned the corner from 1914–1918. The ceremony was held in the onion-domed church of St. Alexandre-Nevsky. Vivienne's employers, Madame and Monsieur Allegre, were our witnesses.

I had sent an invitation to George, but I did not expect him to come. As the ceremony began, however, I heard the creak of the massive door at the other end of the aisle. Somehow I knew it had to be him. He had travelled for four days to reach Biarritz, and he stayed with us for a week before returning to the foothills of the Dentelles. He was older, of course, than when he'd last visited me in prison; and although his clothes were much shabbier than I remembered from his visits, his eyes seemed as bright as ever.

"He's still there, you know, Christian. Waiting."

"Waiting for what?" I replied. We walked along the esplanade du Port-Vieux.

"For you perhaps, Christian. And for death. He is not well. He only has a short time left on this earth." George stopped and turned to face me. The perfect Atlantic roared at his back as he whispered these words into my face.

"He abandoned me a long time ago, George. I just stayed in the same house with him for a while beyond that, that's all."

"Even if you don't go back for his sake, go back for yours. He's getting old."

"We all are, George. Even me. I'm more than twice the age I was when we last went to Sablet on the cart."

I knew as soon as I'd said the words that I was condemning George to an immediate recollection of the moments in that small bar when we'd ordered two beers, and bought a knife while we waited.

"I . . . I—" he began.

I stopped him with a wave of my hand and tried to make amends. "George, let's have this out in the open for once and for all," I said.

"Christian, I need to—" he protested.

"You need to listen, George." I smiled. "You had absolutely nothing to do with what happened to Stephane Pleyben."

"But I bought the knife for you."

"Yes, but if you hadn't, I would probably be dead now instead of him. You saved my life, George. You saved it twice; once by buying me that knife and the second time by insisting on giving evidence for me in Carpentras."

"I wish I could believe you, Christian." There was a quiver in his voice and the lightest spray of tears in his eyes. It might have been the sea, but I doubted it.

"You *can* believe me, George. There's nothing in my life that I regret. I have *lived* because of Vivienne, and I have survived death twice because of you. That's an end to it. Alright?" I held my hand out, to seal the version of history I wanted to convey to this ageing foreman whom I loved as if he, and not Robert Aragon, had been my father. He took my hand and the rain on the sea wind encased our handshake.

"Eugene would be very proud of you," he said, as we sought shelter.

"And of you, George," I replied, as we ducked our heads into the squall.

He boarded the train east some days later. I realised that I had probably seen my great friend for the last time. He was the oldest person I knew, and yet in a way he had retained his youthful freshness and loyalty as an antidote to a changing world, where the value placed on life was a poor stock-market risk. He last wrote to me in May, 1937, and properly predicted that his time on earth was almost done.

Elise Morel knows of my correspondence with you, Christian. She is instructed to convey to you the details of my final resting place if you should ever return to Gigondas. Pay me a visit there, and tell me of your life and your dreams. It has been a pleasure and a privilege to know you and to count you among my friends. I enjoyed your wedding as if you were my own son and I hope that, if nothing else, our friendship has imbued you with the knowledge that time and age mean little, and acquaintance and affection mean almost everything there is to know. Live long, be happy, and never take the love of your wife for granted; but greet it anew every day, as fresh as the first moment you met.

A letter from Elise Morel carried sad news: George Phavorin died on the sixteenth of August, 1937. My heart was shattered. My last real link with the village of Gigondas was gone!

It was almost exactly a year later—to the day—that Vivienne and I decided to leave France. We would travel across the sea to a new world where opportunity and anonymity awaited in America. If the mood of the newspapers that summer were to be believed, then the corner France had turned two years previously had doubled back on itself to a new Europe, where the horror of war loitered again.

"It was like this before 1914," Vivienne said one day as I read the headlines.

They spoke of dark clouds in Germany. Monsieur Allegre had made his fortune in the war. He confidently predicted that the scent of innocent blood hung in the air over all of us, in view of what was happening in Berlin and London and elsewhere. I think that if I had believed that Eugene's death had not been in vain, then perhaps in the summer of 1938 I might have been tempted to stay and play my part. To be frank, I felt that I owed France very little at that point. The intimations from Vivienne's employers that they intended to leave the country before any hostilities began made our decision all the easier.

I had worked at odds and ends since arriving in Biarritz. Mostly I earned money on an irregular basis by gardening for old people or well-to-do folk who loved flowers but hated weeding. It was ironic that I chose outdoor work, cultivating flowers and vegetables, when that was essentially the life I'd run away from. The difference was that now it was entirely my own choice—to toil in the sun or the rain, pitting myself against the seasons and the sea. There was no obligation to conform to any plan or path, or to lose sleep over whether I was a disappointment or a credit to anyone other than myself. There were questions that were still unanswered. But I thought that the further away I got from Montmirail, the closer I was likely to get to their resolution. At least that is what I told myself. We booked passage in August, 1938 to sail out from Lisbon for Liverpool in November. From there, we would board a liner for America.

In the autumn of that year I began to feel ill. It was nothing definite at first, more of an uneasy feeling in the cellar of my stomach. I ran a temperature, but had no vomiting. I was seized with irregular headaches, and although different doctors came to see me, they could find nothing wrong. Nothing physical, that is. The latest physician to see me called in October. He turned to me just as he was about to leave.

"It's really none of my business, Monsieur. But I must ask you something." Doctor Crus was an elderly and honourable gentleman. "My attitude towards illness is, at times, unconventional. I believe in the twin remedies of true love and easy sleep." I did not know what he was driving at. "How have you been sleeping?"

"Not well," I answered.

"Since when?"

"A couple of months now, Doctor."

The kindly physician lit a cigarette and blew the smoke up at the ceiling of the room.

"Since you decided to leave for America?"

I cast my mind back to the day of the decision, and the visit to the shipping office to reserve our tickets.

"Almost to the day, Doctor."

He took another long drag of his cigarette and spoke as he exhaled. "That which is left undone can always be finished. For a time."

I knew what I had to do, and where I had to go.

CHAPTER THIRTEEN

The walls on either side of the gate had begun to crumble. Weeds and ivy did what they liked between the plaster and the old stones. I assumed that after my father had died, Montmirail had been bought by someone who would care for it. Perhaps no one had wanted it. The gates were open but one of them had clearly been in that position for years, because it was bound to the ground by grass and climbing vines which were undisturbed. The house itself was virtually unrecognisable from the place I had left on the day of my graduation. The reddish quality of the stonework was compromised in patches where some growth or weakness had allowed decay to set in. The shutters were all closed, and the front door was unwelcoming and isolated. Behind a stone trough, where once flowers may have grown, there was a clutch of spindly dry brown grass.

In the courtyard to the rear, I was greeted by the sight of the old winepress, overgrown with moss. Discarded tools and implements were welded to the press by rust and time. The massive doors of the cellar were nailed shut by boards that formed an X. Through a gap in the buildings I saw some of the vineyard itself. It was bare of vines. At least a portion of it seemed viable. However, large tracts of it were overgrown, and anyway, since it was winter it was difficult to judge. Somewhere far away dogs barked, but beyond that intrusion I heard only a sad awful silence. I walked to the back door of the house and tried to look in at one of the kitchen windows, but it was caked with dirt and neglect and I could see nothing. I thought I saw a lamplight inside, but was unsure.

It was more likely to be the setting sun refracting through the bones of this deceased house.

I knew that the evening was drawing to a close, and I remembered that I'd promised myself to see the graves. Elise Morel ran the bakery. She would tell me where George was buried, although I presumed he would be laid to rest in the village cemetery. As I turned away from the window, something prompted me to try the handle of the door as I passed. It opened easily. I did not know who owned the property now, and although I was a trespasser, I could not resist stepping into the house where I had been born.

"Who's there?" a voice shouted, from a room further in. "Who's there?"

I hesitated, and started to turn and leave before I frightened the new occupant. The glare of a lamp slowly entered the kitchen. I think I had known when I first heard the voice, but there was no doubt when the figure stepped to the side of the lamp which now reposed on the table.

"Papa," I said. "Don't be afraid, it's only me, Christian." I stepped towards him and allowed him to see my face in the glow of the lamp.

"Christian is dead. He died in prison," he snapped.

"No, no. He didn't die. I'm alive, Papa. So much has happened. But I *am* alive."

"Eugene, you look so well. I have kept some of your clothes upstairs in your room. You must be very tired." He came closer to me now and put his hand to my face. I tried to remember all of the things I had once wanted to say to him. The touch of his hand reminded me of the time he had slapped me out in the yard.

"It's the light, Father. You mustn't be able to see properly by it. You don't realise who I am," I said sharply, in reprimand. He pulled a chair out from the table, and with a wave he invited me to do likewise as he sank down into it.

"We thought you had died at Fort Douaumont. They sent a telegram and I was out in the yard cleaning demi-johns when it arrived. No one, except me really, believed you were still alive, you see—"

"Please, Papa, you must listen. I'm not Eugene, I'm Christian—your youngest son. Don't you see the scar on my face?" I pointed at my left cheek.

"You were one of the lucky ones, Eugene. So many men, and some of them only boys like you, went to their deaths in trenches filled with the stench of the rotting corpses of the ones who went before. How did you escape?" His eyes lit up like a child who needs to hear the end of a bedtime story.

I looked at him now, this sick old man. His hair was longer than I had ever seen it. His eyes were sunken into his head like marbles pushed into soft soil, and he had not shaved in some days, at least. Here and there his facial whiskers were longer than at most other locations, and I sensed that even when he did shave he did not use a mirror. I could not tell whether he was really mistaken as to who I was, or if this were an elaborate game devised to isolate and confuse me. I suppose that it might have been appropriate for me at that moment to deliver an ultimatum to him to recognise me. Perhaps I should have threatened to leave, but I did not do so. The light of the lamp was like a star, plucked from the heavens and balanced between us.

"I survived prison and I've made a life for myself," I said, brushing my shirt with one hand.

"You were lucky. They can do great things with medicine now." He smiled. "When your great-grandfather fought at Napoleon's side, all they had to treat the wounded with were cauterising irons and cognac." He sighed and then looked proudly across the table at me. There were tears of joy in his eyes.

"I've got something to show you," he said. "Wait here."

He compressed his fists and pushed them down onto the wooden table to lever himself out of the chair. He stood and pointed at me, as if telling a dog not to move an inch, and then he left the room leaving the lamp behind him. I glanced around the kitchen and saw that there were plates and cups piled high on the work surface beside the cold-press, where cheese and milk were kept. There was a faint stale smell about the place, which hinted at a combination of neglect and forgetfulness. I could not believe that he was still alive. Since George had told me he was ill, I had presumed him dead shortly thereafter. He had outlived us all, in a way, because even I was not the person I had been when I'd left to face prison. I heard him shuffling back in the darkness.

"Look," he said, as he held a small box in his hand. He opened it and I could see that it was a medal.

"The *Medaille d'Or*?" I asked.

He shook his head and laughed. "No, no, my son, not the *Medaille d'Or*. But the token of your country's gratitude for what you did at Fort Douaumont." He took it from its case and handed it to me.

I turned it over in my hand and then placed it on the table. "It's not mine," I said. "It's Eugene's."

My father reached out and took the medal in his hand again. "No, Eugene, it's not just yours; it's ours."

I searched his expression for any hint that he was engaged on a course of deliberate deception, designed to unnerve me and to put me at a disadvantage; I could find none. I decided to play along for a while at least, to see what I could learn from the situation, whatever the reason for his delusion was.

"And Maman. Where is she?"

He lifted his eyes to stare at me and shook his head.

"She is in the ground, Eugene. Right beside the grave where we buried your summer uniform in a wooden box."

"How did—" I began.

"She died of a broken heart. Her soul was battered with disappointment and destroyed. Your brother murdered her, Eugene. As coldly and as surely as he killed Stephane Pleyben, his actions led directly to her death."

I could not let this accusation go unanswered. "No, no, you must be mistaken," I said, raising my voice slightly. "Surely there was some medical explanation? Had she been ill for long before she died?"

"Your poor mother had been ill for a very long time, Eugene. She suffered from that most common of ailments, weakness of spirit."

"You mean she was ill for some time?"

"Since before I married her, Eugene. The Bretons are a simple people who do not possess the essential ingredients for correct living."

"*Ingredients*? What ingredients?" I asked.

A smile lit up his face as he held the medal between his two thumbs and forefingers, and raised it up like the priest would a host. "Duty, patriotism and obedience." He announced the formula with an air of enthusiasm I did not recall him ever displaying when I was growing up. The mantra, too, was new. I suspected that this was a retrospective analysis of his life, expressed in terms he now wished to ascribe to his own actions and their underlying motivation. I recalled George's account of my mother's funeral, and of how my father had not shed a single tear for her.

"Really?" I spoke with a degree of defiance which would have been impossible in my youth.

"You disagree, Eugene?" He was clearly stung by my scepticism.

"They all sound the same to me," I said.

"The same?"

"Yes, Papa. They are all really just euphemisms for doing what other people expect of you."

"You are very wrong, Eugene. These are the only true virtues, and they should be innate rather than acquired if the breeding is correct."

I allowed myself a moment to take this in. I considered now that he really did believe that I was my older brother, returned years later from the war. But what did his theory, now expressed, mean? Was it that he believed my mother to have been below him in social standing? I already knew this from the way he'd treated her. What more then did it mean?

"Have we all disappointed you so much?"

"Not you, Eugene. You have done everything you can to be true to the family tradition and name. You have fought for your country and now you have returned to Montmirail to continue the work of making wine and honouring our ancestors. I have not been able to work for a few days now and things have been allowed to get behind, but together we will soon retrieve the situation."

"And Christian. What of him? How has it happened that he was put into prison? Did he fail to honour some debt?"

My father's expression bore the marks of a genuine desire to cause me as little distress as possible in imparting the news of my own transgressions to me, so that I now believed, in that moment at least, in his eyes I was Eugene. He rose from the table again and lit a second lamp, and we were as clear as day to each other. As he fumbled for two glass tumblers in a cupboard, he directed me to open a bottle of wine from a dusty group lying in a heap on the stone floor. As he poured, he began the sorry task of telling Eugene about my crime.

"Christian was a murderer, Eugene. We could not have known in advance, but his heart was cold and his head was soft. He murdered Stephane Pleyben. He had come back to face his own people and to make amends for his refusal to fight in the war with you, and with the other sons of Gigondas, in the Somme, in Belgium and in God-knows-how-many other fields of battle. Do you remember him? Pleyben?"

"I think he was married to a schoolteacher," I said.

"Yes, yesss," he hissed. "That's the one. He married a whore, but did not know it either."

"And Christian killed Pleyben?"

"Yes, in cold blood, as he slept in his own bed after journeying for days from the Atlantic. Your brother coveted his wife and was not afraid to kill him for that purpose."

"I heard in the village that Pleyben beat her so badly that she could not have children. Are you sure Christian didn't defend Vivienne against her husband? Could it have happened like that?"

The use of her name provoked my father's rage. "Vivienne—" he said slowly, "was that the whore's name? She should have had the decency to stay away from your brother while he was still her pupil. But no. Lust and irresponsibility drove her to seduction and your brother to murder. He was a disgrace to this family even before then, but that—that was the end for me and for your poor mother. He killed that man in the same way that he killed your dog in a fit of rage with an axe. He was a coward too. The animal had not been ensnared, that was a lie. Your brother was afraid to take his place in this family, and a cheap slut convinced him that his cowardice was admirable." He drank the full glass of wine and began to refill it. "I do not wish to talk of him anymore," he said, coldly.

"And what of George? Does he still load the barrels onto the cart and drive to the station in Sablet?"

My father's eyes narrowed. "Monsieur Phavorin too betrayed Montmirail, my son. He was bribed by someone, I do not know whom, to give evidence at the trial in Carpentras. I assume that your brother promised him some share in our home and lands if he were acquitted. Doubtless feeling guilty for having bought the murder weapon, the poor fool gave evidence. But it was to no avail; a conviction ensued and the murderer went to prison."

"And George?"

"That man was given another chance, by me, to redeem himself. I continued to provide a home for him on our property; and he worked well enough under my guidance for some more years, but he could not leave the past alone."

"How do you mean?"

My father drank some more, and then looked pityingly into the air over my head. "I had suspected him of continuing to maintain contact with the murderer, and I discovered some letters in his lodgings which confirmed the fact. I could not have that. I could not allow that treachery to occur under my own roof, at my expense." He was livid now and the colour of his complexion became crimson with the rage these recollections carried with them. "I *did* not allow it to continue."

I became afraid now of what I was about to hear concerning my oldest and dearest friend and ally. "What happened, Papa?"

"I told Monsieur Phavorin that he was no longer welcome in my home or on our land. I dismissed him and he went to the workhouse in Orange. He did not last too long without my charity." He laughed as he said this, and I was gripped with a desire to physically hurt him in retaliation for the cruelty he had heaped on George. Yet I wanted to know more, so I held myself to a degree of calm and drank some of my wine, almost biting through the glass as I did.

I now knew why George had told me to contact Elise Morel in order to find out where his final resting place was. He would be in a pauper's grave, somewhere in Orange. George had concealed his own banishment from me in the hope, perhaps, that I would be reconciled with my father.

"You have had quite a portion of disappointment, then," I said, with sarcasm. "It might have been so different if I had not gone to war."

"No. No. No," he shouted. "Please do not say those things to me. You are a shining example of what this family could and should have been. You understand the meaning of blood, of sacrifice, of tradition. No, my son, it would never have been any different; these people were weak, small-minded, too intent on the selfish fulfilment of warped ideals.

No, Eugene, you must not blame yourself. We cannot blame ourselves. They lacked, the, the—"

"The ingredients," I offered.

"Yes," he said, decisively. "The ingredients."

There was silence between us for a moment as we drank. I could see through the door behind him that the rest of the house was getting darker. I thought about Vivienne waiting for me in Biarritz, and I reminded myself of the other places I had wanted to see on my visit. It was extraordinary that I found myself in the kitchen of Montmirail drinking with my father, and pretending to be my own deceased brother. This was stranger than anything I had ever experienced because it was so utterly unexpected. Did he really not recognise me? That too was extraordinary. But perhaps it was absolutely necessary for me to find answers to the questions I had asked myself for decades.

"What would have happened if he had not committed a murder or gone to prison?"

Now, for the first time in our conversation, I suspected a flicker of recognition in my father's eyes. Even if his mind was failing, it must have had some lucid intervals during which everything appeared to him as it really was. He took one or two deep breaths, and then began to answer me.

"If he had never become involved with that tramp, then, when he had finished his schooling, for whatever it was worth, he would have been able to take his place in this family, in Montmirail. It would have been difficult to teach him the value of family and tradition, but some years of tutoring would finally have taught him what it is to be of Aragon blood. To understand tradition, Eugene, sometimes it is necessary for the tower of the spirit to be broken down and rebuilt with the bricks in the correct order. He would have married someone worthy of Montmirail, and his son would have carried the hopes of this family on into the next century."

He closed his eyes at the last portion of this speech, as though conjuring a vision of continuity in his mind. Then, suddenly, he looked into my eyes and I felt myself being drawn back through the years to when I was a child and we had argued about the value of education and my reluctance to become his heir.

I stared across the table at him and held my breath. Was he aware of who I was all of this time? Did he have in him the requisite guile and arrogance to address me through the employment of this elaborate device of apparent confusion? I sensed, for an instant, that he was laughing at me with his pronouncements about "ingredients" and rebuilding the tower of the spirit. Was this the ultimate display of contempt for me—to refuse to even acknowledge my existence? I did not know, and yet on one level, I felt sure that such a deception was impossible for him. He had always been so direct, so horribly blunt and obvious in showing his prejudices. Often wrong, but never in doubt was how I remembered my father and his opinions. Like a goat on a mountain, always sure of where to put its hoof next, Robert Aragon had ruled over our family with a confidence which could allow no counterview or alternative vision. However, was there any reason why he could not have changed over the intervening years, as I too had undoubtedly changed? I supposed not.

"I love her and she loves me," I said, with anger in my voice and in my heart.

His withered face refused to acknowledge my declaration by not moving a single muscle or nerve. He stood up and walked to the window and began to wipe clear a patch of dust on it so that he could look out into the yard.

"My hands are not as strong as they were long ago, but I know that between us we can clear the weeds and be ready for next year. I think that next summer or perhaps the summer after that, the name of our family will be inscribed on that gold medal in Paris. ARAGON ET FILS. Will you imagine it? Can you travel with me, Eugene, to the *Concours National des Vins* and claim our rightful place?"

"She saved me from myself," I said to his back. "She took me away from this place and she has made me happy."

He turned and smiled into the light. "And how did you find the Germans? Friendly and amenable, or difficult and sour?"

"Compared to some, they were friendly and amenable," I replied. "At least they did not expect me to be something or someone I am not." I wanted to provoke him, and yet I knew that somehow my words could not succeed in that regard.

He shuffled around the room as though searching for something, but then turned to the door and opened it. Some mosquitoes attracted by the light came into the house with a faint whine of their wings.

"Let's have a look at the cellars," he suggested. "You haven't seen them for years."

He took one of the lamps in his hand and I followed him out into the evening. Behind us, the house groaned. I noticed the slow pace of his feet even more now that we were outside. He coughed as we moved, and I felt that the night air would not allow him to last the winter when it came.

"Nineteen twenty-three was the best year for decades, but we have had a few great years since then, Eugene. We have to make the most of what we have kept because there are new markets now. I think our strength has always been that our wine is consistent, year after year."

When we reached the entrance, my father placed the lamp on a stone to the left of the doors and began to pull at the boards. He worked with the apparent power of a man half his age, but as the boards came away I could see that they had rotted through. I stood and watched as one by one the pieces of those once-great doors crumbled in his hands. He talked as he toiled.

"We can sell what we have kept. The money will buy that new strain of vine. The one that Algerian bastard at La Mavette won the regional award with last year."

His pace quickened now and he flailed away at the remaining boards. As he did, a stench was set free. The opening became fully exposed. I lifted the lamp, fearing what I was about to see revealed in its light. Hundreds, perhaps thousands, of bottles lay smashed on the floor of the cellars as far in as the eye could see. The rancid odour was like the scent of hell itself, and it enveloped us in the frightening grip of dead wine—this vile adulterated smell of a decaying family. A carpet of green and blue mould sat on the surface of the scene, but through this coat of slime and age, thousands of pieces of broken glass peered up at us. It might have been a decade in this condition, I could not tell. But I did know, in an instant, that this scene was not the product of either accident or neglect. I lifted the lamp higher and saw a little further into the throat of the cellars. The two huge barrels built to the right of the first hallway clearing had been smashed beyond use, so that their contents too had joined the carnage and flooded the remainder of the oldest cellars in Provence.

"It's true what they say; wine definitely improves with age." He began to laugh maniacally.

It was as though this was the punch line in a terrible story or joke which he had been enjoying all my life. I had been shocked to learn that he was still alive. But perhaps even more disturbing was this apparent charade he had engaged in since my chance arrival at Montmirail less than an hour before. He could not have anticipated ever meeting me again, and yet he seemed to be rehearsed in his behaviour and attitude. Was it part madness, part lucidity, and part history which had lain in wait for my return? He had disowned me before the trial. He never contacted me after my conviction. He had punished George for showing me the type of love and support he himself seemed incapable of. Now, upon my return, he had vilified my mother, denigrated my wife and flatly refused to even recognise me, preferring instead to mock me as my own brother.

And my response? I had indulged him in his macabre fantasy and had been whisked back into short trousers, and the ebb and flow of childhood, to be reprimanded like a boy and laughed at like a fool. I wanted to hurt him. Part of me even thought of killing him with my bare hands, to wring out of his old body some of the retribution I sought for the ineffectiveness of my mother, the loss of my brother, and the humiliation heaped on a loyal foreman simply because he had written to me in prison. He had beaten me on many occasions, and I knew that he had enjoyed it. I realised that for the first time in my life I was not afraid of him. If we came to blows now I knew that I would not be defeated by him.

How dare he try, in the twist of a few sentences, to dismiss the love that I had shared with Vivienne for almost two decades despite the adversity we had faced? Who was Robert Aragon to drag me back to sixteen years of age and condemn my entire life, just because of his own disappointments? I wanted to do something that would shake the bitterness out of him, or at least convey to him the final truth of life: death stalks us all and each of us is only the sum of our own failures and successes. It is nothing more or less than that.

"George Phavorin was more of a father to me than you could ever have been in a thousand years."

Those words formed in my mind, but something stopped me from speaking them. From somewhere else, some rippling of change wooed my soul and made me think again. Perhaps it was the hint of the future I was now going to enjoy, I have no idea. Maybe it was my past, finally allowing me to let it go. Perhaps it was just something inside of me which had changed or grown up. Or forgiven itself.

"There's a push on at the front starting tomorrow, Papa. I'm due back with my unit in the next day or two, so I'm afraid I can't stay."

He looked at me in the lamplight and placed a hand on my shoulder. "I think there are things which are more important to you than even the *Medaille d'Or*?" His voice suddenly seemed to lose its former trace of bitterness.

"I suppose that's the truth of it, really," I said, handing him the lamp.

I looked at my father for the last time and began to turn away. I could hear him humming to himself, and methodically kicking the rotten boards and door-pieces into a heap in rhythm with his own tune. I walked across the yard past the rusted winepress. I saw the light of the other lamp in the kitchen, although it was beginning to dim as the oil ran low. At the front of the house, I made my way slowly down the tree-lined avenue to the open gates. On my way into the village, I stepped off the road at one point and cut a small shoot from a vine to take with me on my journey. The earth was slightly hard beneath my feet, and I felt compassion for those varieties of crops or people which cannot flourish here in the heat and the poor soil. I saw the faint outline of those large pudding-shaped rocks which do their best to reflect the efforts of their masters back at them. I felt the chill of November swirl around me, but it left me no less warm inside. I continued up through the village and saw a light over a low wall.

In the main street I stood in front of the bakery. In my mind and in my heart I saw the ghosts of a boy and his dog still waiting. Couderc smiled and they retreated. I knocked on the door. Elise Morel came out from the kitchen, wiping flour from her hands. As she undid the lock I watched her with peace in my soul, and prepared myself to tell her what had happened to me since that hot July in 1920 had baked us all and turned children into men and women.

Epilogue

Maybe others would have acted differently had they been in my shoes. That house, and the village which insulates it from the Dentelles, are part of a way of life that I have rejected. The day Eugene died changed my life forever, although I did not realise it at the time. I wonder if he is up there somewhere, making judgments about my actions and choices. It is impossible to know whether there is another life beyond this earthly one. In a way, that does not really matter, because I know that I would not have lived my own life any differently even if I knew one way or another for certain.

When I think of Gigondas and the summer of 1920, I cannot be sad. As the propellers of this huge ship churn beneath the surface of the black Atlantic, and my wife sleeps in our tiny cabin on the lowest of six decks, I feel that the best part of my life lies ahead. I am glad that I returned to Gigondas to make my peace with the past. There are portions of my life there that I will carry with me forever. Over the sound of the sea I can hear the gurgle of the water in the Place de la Fontaine, the tired sighs of the mayor avoiding his wife by overworking, the rasp of the chairs on the terrace outside the hotel, and the excited prattle of children on a half-day from school. In my dreams, I can fly once more.

I AM reminded of the day I'd been released from prison. We had made our way through the morning streets of Marseille. I tasted freedom and breathed in fresh air and heard the chatter of people who meant me no harm. We held hands like teenage lovers, linking fingers and knowing that the symbolism of that gesture led the way to something much more passionate and intimate. It began to rain just as we reached her abode on the Rue Haxo. Vivienne unlocked the door. I was shocked by her action of making her way ahead of me into the rooms. In prison I was always forced to walk first through the unlocked door or gate, because the person with the key would have to lock it behind me.

In the bedroom, a razor and shaving soap had been laid out for my use beside the ewer of water. I shaved with the aid of a small mirror. As I lifted the razor, I saw Vivienne standing behind me as I looked in the mirror. She wore an expression I could not decipher.

"Does my appearance frighten you?" I asked.

"No." She laughed. "It's just that there's someone handsome in there behind all of that hair, and I'm anxious to see him again." I continued my soapy task.

"Thank you," she said, putting her arms around my waist from behind as I shaved.

"For what?"

"For risking your life to save mine. For pleading guilty to a crime you did not commit, just to save me from the guillotine."

"It was nothing," I said, and I meant it. I would have done the same thing again that very day if I had had to.

"You know sometimes I'm sorry, Christian, that I did not insist on giving evidence. I could have—"

"You could have ruined everything, Chérie. You could have stood up there and told the truth, and then where would we have been? You would have been dead, and without you I would be as good as dead."

Vivienne began to cry softly. I held her, then I finished shaving. The symbolism of the razor was not lost on us. When she'd taken the knife from my hands and ended Stephane's days, she had given new life to both of us. We had watched her horrible husband die, and our complicity in that act of watching would bind us forever. We had had little enough time to decide what to do next, and strange as it may seem, it was I who had taken the initiative.

"Change your clothes and bury them in the woods," I instructed Vivienne. "You will have to go and find the doctor and bring him here."

"And what will you do, Christian? Surely it would be better to pack our things and try to get as far away from here as we can?"

Vivienne's blouse was stained with blood and one particular portion of the stain resembled the outline of a face. That was the moment for me to grow up and I did my best to do it.

"No. No. If we run, they'll follow us and we'll both be sent to the guillotine. We must stay and see this through. Leterrier knows we were here with your husband. He will make sure we are tracked down and killed if we try to escape. I will take the blame. *You* must say you saw nothing."

"But, Christian," she screamed. "I've killed him, we must—"

"We must stay. You fetch the doctor. Tell him your husband is dead. We must decide on what to say and not waver from that version of events. Do you understand me?"

"But why should I say I did not witness the struggle? Surely it would be better if I said you killed him to save my life?"

I shook my head. "No. No. If you say you were here, then we will both be charged. If you are found guilty, you will certainly be executed. You must say you were somewhere else, outside at the well, anywhere, just not here. I am little more than a child to the law. Whatever chance we have of being together, it is only if I take the blame. Do you understand?"

I took her hands in mine and wiped the blood from them onto my face. Time would be of the essence if the priest had spoken to anyone since arriving back in the village. Of all people, he could not be relied upon to keep his mouth shut. Vivienne took a deep breath and began to undress. After she had changed, she looked at the corpse with its glazed eyes and blood splatters. She took her stained clothes with her and hesitated at the door as she opened it. She was about to protest again, but I spoke first.

"You were outside and came back and found me here, and Stephane dead. That is your story. Do not deviate from it. Leave the rest to me. Alright?"

When I was nine years old, a boy at school cut me on the left side of my face with a hunting knife in a fight about nothing. When I was almost seventeen, a pocket-knife cut me free in a fight about absolutely everything. I carry all of my scars with pride and hope. This is who I am.

"I love you, Christian," she mouthed silently, as she opened the door. She stepped out into the future. The rest you know.